The sky was filled with exploding fireworks, and the party moved to the upper deck, crowding around the railing facing the harbor. Sue woke and, guessing that her greenish pallor was not the reflection of the fireworks, Lucy helped her up and led her downstairs.

"Don' fee-el goo'," said Sue.

"Look at the fireworks," urged Lucy, hoping to distract her.

Sue clutched the railing and leaned over. *Here we go,* thought Lucy. But she was wrong; Sue was pointing to the water.

"Whaash that?"

Lucy looked down and saw something white. "A reflection?"

"No." Sue leaned over farther, and Lucy grabbed the back of her dress.

"Whoa, there. You're going to fall in."

"Thas wha' happened. Somebody fell in."

Lucy looked again. Sue was right. Whatever was floating there did resemble a human shape.

"It's probably garbage or something," said Lucy, looking up as a giant rocket exploded overhead, filling the sky with light.

"Not garbage." Sue tugged her sleeve. "Look."

Lucy looked and saw the white form now had arms and legs and a head, all floating a few inches below the surface of the water. Another wave came and the body rolled over. Even in the dim light, Lucy was sure it was Ron. . . .

Books by Leslie Meier

MISTLETOE MURDER
TIPPY TOE MURDER
TRICK OR TREAT MURDER
BACK TO SCHOOL MURDER
VALENTINE MURDER
CHRISTMAS COOKIE MURDER
TURKEY DAY MURDER
WEDDING DAY MURDER
BIRTHDAY PARTY MURDER

Published by Kensington Books

A Lucy Stone Mystery

WEDDING DAY MURDER

Leslie Meier

KENSINGTON BOOKS
Kensington Publishing Corp.
http://www.kensingtonbooks.com

KENSINGTON BOOKS are published by

Kensington Publishing Corp.
850 Third Avenue
New York, NY 10022

All Kensington Titles, Imprints, and Distributed Lines
are available at special quantity discounts for bulk pur-
chases for sales promotions, premiums, fund-raising,
and educational or institutional use. Special book ex-
cerpts or customized printings can also be created to fit
specific needs. For details, write or phone the office of
the Kensington special sales manager: Kensington
Publishing Corp., 850 Third Avenue, New York, NY
10022, attn: Special Sales Department, Phone: 1-800-
221-2647.

Kensington and the K logo Reg. U.S. Pat. & TM Off.

First Hardcover Printing: November 2001
First Paperback Printing: June 2002
10 9 8 7 6 5 4 3 2

Printed in the United States of America

Chapter One

Standing in her kitchen in Tinker's Cove, Maine, where she was cooking up a big pot of clam chowder base she planned to freeze for easy summer suppers, Lucy Stone knew she was in the final countdown. The hands on the old Regulator clock read a quarter past three; in moments the school bus would arrive for the last time until next September. It was Monday, June 17—the last day of school.

Watching the second hand jump forward, Lucy felt her freedom ticking away. Oh, she'd had a better run than usual this year. Thanks to several heavy snowstorms, the school calendar had been extended to make up the lost days. But now, the 180 days mandated by the Tinker's Cove school board and agreed to by the teacher's union had finally been completed.

The grind of gears as the big yellow school bus started the climb up Red Top Road told Lucy her time had run out. This must be what it feels like to be a condemned prisoner who hears her last appeal has been denied, she thought. She went over to the screen door and listened. It was like this every year; she could hear the children's excited screams as the bus drew closer. Then the brakes squealed and the doors flapped open.

"Talk about your cold-blooded killers," said Geoff Rumford, pointing at a bowl full of seashells Lucy had set on the table as a centerpiece, "nothing beats your humble moon snail."

Lucy glanced around the dining room table where they were gathered and then looked at the bowl of seashells she had used for a centerpiece. She had taken extra care setting the table, not only because Geoff was a guest, but because it was the first time in a long time that the whole family had been able to eat together and she had wanted to make it special.

"I've always thought moon snails are pretty," she said, studying the bleached white shells. She picked one up, noticing its satisfying round shape and the neat, concentric whorl of dark gray on one side. It was as if an artist had taken a fine brush and added the subtlest swirl of color to emphasize the snail's shape.

"This snail doesn't look like much of a threat to me," she added, smiling broadly at Geoff. Geoff always made her smile. He was young—in his late-twenties—and good-looking, but that was only part of it. It was also that she so wholeheartedly approved of Geoff. He was a graduate of the local high school in Tinker's Cove and had gone on to college and was now working on his doctorate in marine biology at Columbia University in New York City. He was a young man with bright prospects—exactly the sort of young person she hoped her own four children would turn out to be.

"Not a threat to you, but believe me, pretty terrifying to a scallop or clam." Geoff winked at Zoe, at six years of age the youngest of Lucy's children, and started humming the shark theme from *Jaws*.

"That's right," chimed in Toby, at eighteen the oldest, who had just finished his freshman year at Coburn University in New Hampshire. He was spending his summer vacation working for Geoff, helping with his thesis project. "The moon snail has a special organ called a radula which it uses to drill right through the shell of a poor, helpless little blue-eyed scallop."

Sara, who was thirteen and a champion of all animals, gulped hard.

"The scallop can't get away," continued Toby, smiling rather meanly. "It just has to sit there while the moon snail drills away at its shell."

"What happens then?" asked Elizabeth, directing her question at Geoff. She was seventeen and would continue her education in the fall at Chamberlain College in Boston. In the meantime, she was looking for more excitement than her summer job as a chambermaid at the Queen Victoria Inn could offer.

"Uh, well," replied Geoff, growing a bit red around the collar, "the snail sucks out the clam and eats it for dinner. Just like we're doing. This chowder is delicious."

"Lucy's a great cook—when she bothers to take the time," said Bill, from his seat at the head of the table.

That's how it was with Bill these days, she thought. Always that note of criticism. She'd first noticed it last fall, when he was out of work for a few weeks. He'd promptly gotten another job and their finances had soon recovered, but not Bill's spirits. Hopefully it was just a temporary phase, a little bout of insecurity. She hoped so; she was tired of constantly struggling to keep her temper—not that she always managed to succeed.

"What time?" she asked, her voice rising in pitch. "Between work and the kids' schedules, there's no time to make dinner from scratch." She looked at her husband. "Now that school's out, I'm hoping we can have more family dinners."

Bill's expression was doubtful. "Since you're working full-time, how's that going to happen? It's going to be pizza, pizza, hamburgers and more pizza."

Lucy changed the subject. "Would anyone like seconds?"

"Don't mind if I do," said Geoff, passing his bowl over for a refill.

"So, Geoff," said Bill, passing his bowl, too. "What is this research project all about, anyway? Not snails, I bet."

"Not snails. Lobsters. As I'm sure you know, there's been a sudden drop in the population and I want to find out why."

"I thought it was overfishing," said Lucy, who worked as a reporter at the local weekly newspaper and was familiar with the problem. Declining catches and increased regulations had brought the industry to near collapse, and tensions were running high on the waterfront as fishermen, some of whom were the sons and grandsons of seafaring men, saw their traditional way of life threatened.

"Well, that's part of the problem, but the fishermen say they're seeing a lot more sick and diseased lobsters that they can't sell. If we can find out what's going on, we may be able to keep the stock healthier."

"What does it matter?" asked Sara, with a resigned sigh. "They'll kill them anyway."

"It's jobs, silly," said Toby, his voice weary with the weight of the knowledge and sophistication he'd acquired in his freshman year. "This is Maine. Lobsters are big business."

"Well, I don't think it makes any difference to the lobsters," Sara answered self-righteously.

A honk sounded in the driveway and she jumped to her feet.

"Where do you think you're going?" demanded Bill.

"The movies. Mom said it was okay."

"I did? I don't remember that."

"You know. With Jessica and Caitlin and Meghan. I haven't seen them since school got out a whole week ago."

"I must have forgotten," said Lucy.

Bill looked to Geoff for sympathy. "If I had a dollar for everything she's forgotten lately . . ."

"Who's driving?" asked Lucy.

"Caitlin's mom. And she's bringing us home, too."

"Okay. But remember you have to get up early tomorrow." Sara and Zoe both went to the day camp at the local Friends of Animals shelter, and Sara was a counselor-in-training. It was the cheapest camp Lucy could find, but the girls' camp fees were the main reason Lucy had switched from part-time to full-time at the paper.

Sara ran out, letting the screen door slam behind her.

"I don't know why we can't ever seem to have a family dinner anymore," grumbled Bill. "When I was a kid, my mom made . . ."

"Things have changed so much since then," teased Lucy, determined not to be drawn into a fight. She knew Bill didn't want her working at all. If he had his druthers, she'd be a full-time housewife like his mother was. "Take electricity and indoor plumbing, for example."

Bill grimaced at her but didn't say anything.

"So what exactly will you and Toby be doing?" asked Elizabeth, fixing her dark eyes on Geoff and twirling a lock of her short, dark hair around her finger. "How will you actually conduct the research?"

"Just like the lobstermen, with one big difference. We'll trap the critters and log their condition, draw some blood, and then we'll return them to the water."

"There must be more to it than that," insisted Elizabeth, batting her eyelashes.

Watching her daughter's performance, Lucy hoped she wasn't going to spend the summer throwing herself at everyone she met who happened to wear pants.

"Oh, there is," said Geoff, sitting up a little straighter in his chair. "We have to analyze the blood, identify any parasites, and write up the results."

"It sounds fascinating," cooed Elizabeth, propping her chin on her elbow and leaning toward Geoff.

"It is pretty interesting, actually," said Geoff, his lips curling into a smile.

"Aren't you going out or something tonight?" asked Toby, irritated that Geoff was paying so much attention to his sister.

"Not until six-thirty."

"It *is* six-thirty," said Toby.

"Shit!" exclaimed Elizabeth, jumping up.

"Watch your language," admonished Bill.

"Uh, sorry. I've got to go," she said, pausing to sway her hips provocatively as she passed Geoff.

"Better not keep your date waiting," said Geoff.

"It's not a date—she's just going to the mall with Jenny," said Toby.

"Don't act like you know who I'm going out with because you don't," said Elizabeth. "Besides, it's none of your business."

"It is if you're planning to take the truck, because I'm going to need it later."

"Can't Eddie pick you up for once?" said Elizabeth, giving tit for tat.

"No, he can't. Besides, I got permission from Dad."

Bill nodded and handed the keys over to Toby.

Elizabeth appealed to her mother. "Mom, can I borrow your car?"

"I guess so." Hearing the phone ring, she added, "Get that, please."

"Sure thing." A moment later, she was back. "It's for Zoe."

"For me?" Zoe was delighted. Although the phone seemed to ring constantly for her older siblings, it was rarely for her.

"Just say you have to call back because it's dinnertime," said Lucy, invoking a nearly forgotten family rule.

"Do I have to?"

Lucy looked around at the empty places at the table and decided she was fighting a losing battle.

"Just this once," she said, relenting. "I don't know why I bothered to make dessert if nobody's here to eat it."

"Dessert?" Bill was definitely interested.

"Strawberry-rhubarb pie."

"Homemade?"

Lucy wasn't about to admit she'd bought it at the grocery store. "Let's have our pie and coffee in the gazebo," she said.

The gazebo was tucked in beside the house, in a spot that was secluded from the road but still had a view of the green, tree-covered mountains in the distance.

"Wow," said Geoff when he saw the structure for the first time. "This is really something."

The trim, white summerhouse was indeed a triumph of the builder's craft, constructed last fall by Bill when a job fell through and he had time on his hands. He was a restoration carpenter and he'd used his knowledge of Victorian architecture to create a fanciful little jewel complete with a pagoda-style roof and plenty of gingerbread trim.

"I just love it," said Lucy, who was carrying a tray loaded with pie, dessert dishes, and mugs of coffee. She was keeping a watchful eye on the dog, Kudo, who had trotted up hopefully as soon as they appeared in the yard. He was a sociable mutt, but Lucy suspected he was primarily interested in snagging some pie.

"Want me to tie him up?" asked Bill, who was carrying the cream and sugar.

"Oh, no. He'll be good," said Lucy, who hated to see a dog tied.

"Not so far." Bill nodded at the dog, who had buried his nose in Geoff's crotch.

"Don't mind him," said Lucy with an embarrassed giggle. "It's just his way of saying hello." She set the tray down on the table and seated herself in a wicker chair.

"If you ignore him, he'll lose interest," she advised Geoff, who was vainly attempting to push the dog away.

"Kudo! Stop that!" bellowed Bill.

The dog turned around to give Bill a questioning glance, and Geoff seized the opportunity to escape.

"Lucy, I've told you before, you've got to train that dog."

"I'll add it to the list."

"Well, if you wouldn't insist on working at that newspaper, you'd have plenty of time for some projects this summer," said Bill.

"My main project is going to be spending a few pleasant hours out here," said Lucy, cutting the pie. She tossed a piece of crust to Kudo, who swallowed it whole in one gulp.

He sat politely, staring at the pie, mutely suggesting that he could stand a tad more.

"No," she told him.

With a sigh, he settled down and rested his chin on his paws.

"This is incredible," said Geoff, tilting his head back to admire the intricate joinery.

"I've always dreamed of having a gazebo," said Lucy. "I love coming out here. It's just a few feet from the house, but somehow it seems as if it's miles from everything. No phone. No TV. It's so peaceful."

"Can you see the sunset from here?"

"You betcha," said Bill, lifting a forkful of pie to his mouth. "That's why I put it here."

"We have beautiful sunsets, with the mountains and all," added Lucy.

"That's one of the things I miss in New York," said Geoff, leaning back in his chair. "I mean, I'm sure they have great sunsets with the Hudson River and the Palisades and all, but I've never actually seen one. I always seem to be stuck in a classroom or a lab or in the subway."

"So you chose a research project that allowed you to come back home?"

"It was a no-brainer," said Geoff. "Besides, my grant isn't too big, so I'm on a pretty tight budget. This way I can keep costs low by bunking with Fred."

Lucy and Bill both knew Fred Rumford, Geoff's older brother, who was a professor of archaeology at nearby Winchester College. He was currently excavating a Native American burial site on Andy Brown's farm.

"We really appreciate that you hired Toby," said Bill. "It's a great opportunity for him."

"He's a super kid," said Geoff. "He's going to earn his wages, though. I plan to work him hard."

"Good," said Bill.

"Send him home too tired to eat," added Lucy.

"I'll do my best," said Geoff. "I haven't forgotten some of the stunts I pulled when I was his age. It's amazing no one got hurt. Why, I remember one night when I went over to Gideon with some other guys to buy booze. The idea was nobody'd recognize us over there so they'd sell it to us, and then we'd bring it back and have a party at Chuck Swift's house because his folks were away. Problem was, we started drinking on the drive home and got so drunk we never did find our way back. We ended up parking and sleeping it off in the woods. I caught hell for that one."

"Nowadays, you'd probably end up spending the night in jail," said Bill. "They've really cracked down on underage drinking."

"Good thing, too," said Geoff. "I saw Chuck at the harbor. He's pulling lobsters for a living and he's married to Carrie Eldredge. They have a little girl."

"I typed up the birth announcement for the paper," said Lucy. "One of the few we get these days. Most of the kids leave as soon as they graduate from high school."

"Frank Wiggins is still here," said Geoff. "He's the harbormaster."

Lucy rolled her eyes. "He's one of the ones who should have left, if you ask me."

"What's the matter with Frank?"

"You'll find out soon enough. He's not making a lot of friends in his new job."

"Really? He seems like a natural for the job. Wasn't his dad the harbormaster?"

"Sure was. And his uncle's chairman of the waterways commission," said Lucy.

"And the rest of the members are his cousins," added Bill.

Geoff laughed. "Small-town politics. Some things never change."

"I love Tinker's Cove," said Lucy. "It's been a great place to raise a family, but I hope our kids will follow your example and move on to a place with more opportunities."

"I dunno," said Geoff. "I'm really not a city person. It's awfully nice to be back. Besides, with computers and high-tech communication, people can live just about anywhere and have great careers."

"Talk about great careers—have you heard about Sidra Finch?"

"What about Sidra?" asked Geoff in a carefully casual voice.

"She works on the Norah Hemmings TV talk show. She's a producer in New York." Lucy remembered something. "Didn't I hear you two were dating?"

"I saw her once or twice," admitted Geoff.

"Then I guess you know she's engaged."

For a moment, Geoff looked as if he'd been punched in the stomach, but he quickly recovered. "How wonderful for her," he said.

"Her folks are really excited," continued Lucy, who counted Sidra's mother, Sue Finch, among her closest friends. "Especially Sue, of course. They haven't even set the date yet, but she's already planning the wedding."

"Is that so?" asked Geoff, standing and walking over to the railing, where he stood for a moment, apparently admiring the view. "I'd love to stay longer, but I've really got to go. Thanks for everything."

"Anytime," said Bill.

Together, he and Lucy walked Geoff to the driveway, where they saw him off in his aged Toyota.

"He's a great guy," said Bill. "I hope Toby doesn't let him down."

"What do you mean?" asked Lucy.

"Oh, kids today, they're not used to physical work. Don't have much backbone."

"Toby's a hard worker. Besides, this job is bound to be interesting. It's a research project, after all."

Bill looked at her. "Sometimes I don't know what's come over you," he said, scratching his beard. "When we moved here, we agreed we wanted to live simply. Remember? We were going to work with our hands and be as self-sufficient as possible? Now, it seems all you can talk about is sending the kids to college so they can have fancy jobs in some crowded, filthy city."

"Don't you want them to go to college?" Lucy was shocked.

"Sure. But you seem to have the idea that they've got to have big, important careers. There's nothing wrong with living right here, you know. Working with their hands or something." He looked down and started working at the gravel in the driveway with his foot.

"I never said there was anything wrong with working with their hands."

"You want them to do better than us. To make more money. You think I'm a failure."

Lucy was stunned. She couldn't believe what she was hearing. "That's not true. You're an artist—just look at the gazebo. I wish I had a tenth of your skill and talent."

"Skill and talent don't count for much when there isn't any work."

"You lost one job, Bill, and that was last fall. You're

working now; you've got contracts lined up for the future. We're doing fine financially."

"Then why are you working full-time?"

"The day camp is expensive. . . ."

"Why do they have to go to day camp? Why can't they spend the summer swimming and boating and picking berries, the way they used to?"

"I wish they could," said Lucy, "but times have changed. All their friends are at day camp and that's where they want to go, too."

"I don't like it," said Bill, shaking his head. "We've lost something here and it's really too bad."

Lucy stood in the driveway, watching as he walked back to the house. His step lacked its usual spring. He wasn't getting any younger, she thought. His temples were touched with gray and his beard, once a rich chestnut color, was now grizzled. Maybe he was feeling his age. Maybe it was that male midlife crisis she'd heard so much about. Whatever it was, she hoped he'd get over it soon. She started to follow him, then remembered the dirty dishes in the gazebo and went on around the house.

It was still too early for the sunset, but a few pink clouds were hovering above the dark, shadowy mountains. Lucy paused to admire the view, then started stacking the dishes on the tray. She had finished and was starting back to the house, carrying the tray, when she remembered the pie.

They'd only eaten three pieces; there was at least half a pie left. But where was it? Not on the table where she'd left it, that was for sure. Noticing movement out of the corner of her eye, Lucy turned and caught a glimpse of Kudo's bushy tail as he disappeared into the woods. On the ground a few feet away was the empty pie plate.

"Bad dog!" she yelled, venting her frustration. If she were keeping score, she thought, she'd have to admit she was on a losing streak. In just one evening she'd failed to hold the family together for one complete meal; she'd tactlessly questioned her son's boss about his love life; she'd apparently alienated her husband; and it was only a matter of time before she had a very sick dog on her hands. If this kept up, it was going to be a very long summer.

Chapter Two

As Lucy zipped up the last of five lunch bags, she wondered why they called it summer vacation. It certainly wasn't a vacation for her. This morning, for instance, she had pulled on her khaki slacks but hadn't yet had time to take off her nightgown before Kudo began demanding to be let out. Considering the amount of pie he'd devoured the night before, she didn't think she ought to make him wait. Then she'd been caught up in a whirlwind of small tasks: making lunches, finding missing articles of clothing, coaxing Elizabeth and Toby out of bed.

Come to think of it, Sara and Zoe were the only ones enjoying a vacation this summer, whiling away the long days at day camp. But as far as Lucy could tell, day camp was turning out to be a lot like school, except for the fact that public school was free and day camp cost money and didn't provide bus service. The way things were turning out, she was spending an awful lot of time chauffeuring the kids around.

Toby and Elizabeth both had driver's licenses, but they didn't have cars of their own. Every penny that they earned from their summer jobs was needed for college expenses. Lucy had the Subaru wagon and Bill had a pickup truck, and they both needed their vehicles for work. There was no such thing as public transportation in Tinker's Cove, so that meant the kids had to be driven to their summer jobs. Lucy glanced at the Regulator clock on the wall, took a quick slug of coffee, and dashed upstairs. She had five minutes to finish getting dressed before she had to be on the road.

First stop was the Friends of Animals day camp, then on to the Queen Victoria Inn, where Elizabeth would be ten minutes late for work.

"Mom, I really don't see why you can't drop me off first—Mrs. McNaughton always gives me a hard time about being late."

"Because it would mean backtracking five or six miles, that's why. Listen, Elizabeth, I can't be in two places at once. You have to be at work at eight; the girls have to be at camp at eight. It's as simple as that. Just explain the situation to Mrs. McNaughton. I'm sure she'll understand."

"You don't know what she's like, Mom."

"I'll give her a call and explain."

Elizabeth's eyes widened in horror. "Don't do that—promise?"

Lucy pulled up in front of the inn and braked. "Whatever."

Elizabeth got out of the car, slammed the door, and ran up the porch stairs. Lucy drove on.

"What was that all about?" she asked Toby, who was slumped beside her in the front passenger seat.

"Whuh?" he grunted, rubbing his eyes.

"How do you do it? How can you sleep in the car with the radio going and your sisters talking?"

"I dunno."

Lucy shook her head. She remembered touring the Coburn University campus with Toby and reading the words inscribed on the library doors: "You are the hope of the world."

The world, she decided as she pulled up at the wharf, was in trouble.

"Have a nice day," she told him as he unfolded himself from the car.

"Yo," he said.

Lucy sped off across the parking lot and stopped at the corner of Sea Street. It was then she noticed his lunch, forgotten on the car floor. Sighing, she made an illegal U-turn and headed back to the waterfront. Toby was gone, of course, so she had to park the car in order to look for him.

Walking back across the parking lot to the wharf, lunch bag in hand, she enjoyed the warmth of the sun on her face. It was a beautiful summer day, but she'd been too busy to notice. She sniffed the distinctive scent of saltwater, fish, and diesel fuel and resolved to slow down and smell the . . . well, maybe not roses, but it was still summer and she was lucky enough to live in one of the most beautiful spots in the whole world. She stopped in her tracks and looked out across the little round harbor, where the colorfully painted boats bobbed at anchor, to the pine-covered hills on the other side. There was absolutely nothing lovelier, she decided, than the dark-green color of a pine tree meeting a clear blue sky; there was no sound wilder and freer than the call of a soaring herring gull.

Lucy was about to step onto the town dock when she noticed the "Authorized Persons Only" sign and paused. This was something new, and she didn't like it. She'd never had to get authorization to go on the dock before. She'd always been able to just walk out and get to whatever boat she needed to get to. And who exactly was she supposed to get authorization from? The sign went on to say "By Order of the Harbormaster." Was she actually supposed to go all the way over to the harbormaster's shack and get permission to walk out a few yards on the dock to Geoff's boat, the Lady L?

She didn't think so. Squaring her shoulders, she marched right past the sign and on out to the Lady L's berth. There she saw Toby bent over the engine.

"You forgot your lunch," she yelled.

Toby looked up, eyebrows raised.

"Your lunch." She held up the bag.

Recognition dawned.

"Thanks, Mom." He straightened up and leaned across the small gap between boat and dock, taking the bag from her.

"So this is the boat," she said, taking in the Lady L from stem to stern. It was just an ordinary Down East lobster boat with a three-sided wheelhouse and a winch for hauling lobster pots up from the sea bottom. "Somehow I thought a research boat would be bigger or something."

"Nope. It's just for catching lobsters. Geoff has a lab on shore, at the college."

"Oh. Makes sense."

"Yeah. Well, thanks, Mom. I've got to get back to work."

"Right. See you tonight."

She started back toward the parking lot, taking care on the floating walkway that rocked under her feet, when she heard voices. She looked up and saw Geoff and Frank Wiggins, the harbormaster, standing at the end of the walkway by the new sign. She raised her arm and waved, but the two men didn't notice her. They were too busy arguing.

"That's ridiculous," she heard Geoff say in an exasperated tone. "It doesn't make any sense."

"Listen here," said Wiggins, pausing to spit in the water, "you may be some big shot in the city, but around here I'm the boss."

He blinked a few times for emphasis and twisted his face into a leer.

As she approached, Lucy couldn't help thinking that Wiggins was a remarkably odd-looking man. He was stick-thin and his blue harbormaster's uniform hung on his boney, hunched frame. His overlarge head was perched on a skinny neck, where his Adam's apple bulged out. It seemed to have a life of its own, twitching and bobbing about in his poorly shaved neck. His face would have been unremarkable enough, except for the fact that he had decided to embellish it with a luxurious gunfighter's mustache, which drooped several inches down on either side of his mouth. The mustache did help to cover his discolored and uneven teeth, but it was hardly a thing of beauty in its own right, stained as it was with nicotine and coffee and whatever the man had eaten at his last meal.

"What I say goes," he asserted, thrusting his face at Geoff's. "Got that?"

Geoff sighed in frustration. "I'm trying to help you out here, you know. I'm not the only one who's affected by this. When the other guys hear about this you're going to have a mutiny on your hands."

Lucy's reportorial nose sniffed a story. "Nice day," she said, and both men turned toward her. Geoff took the opportunity to get back to his boat, giving her a nod as he passed her on the walkway.

"What's he all steamed up about?" she asked Wiggins.

"That's between him and me," said Wiggins, turning his red-rimmed eyes on Lucy. "Didn't you see the sign?"

"I was just taking my son his lunch," she explained. "He's on the Lady L with Geoff."

"That happens again, you come to me first. You gotta get authorization, see?"

From the sound issuing from his throat, Lucy was pretty sure he was going to spit again.

"I'll do that," she said, hurrying past him.

When she arrived at the *Pennysaver* office, no one else was there. No wonder, she thought, it was only eight-thirty. Phyllis, the part-time receptionist, usually arrived around nine, and Ted, the publisher and editor-in-chief, rarely made it in before nine-thirty. Lucy got the coffeepot started and booted up her computer. As she reviewed her story budget for the week, she decided to ask Ted if he'd be interested in having her write a story about Geoff's lobster research project. He was always encouraging her to come up with "in-depth" stories, and the lobster project seemed ideal, especially considering the impact lobsters had on the local economy.

She poured herself a cup of coffee and sipped it, wondering what Geoff and Wiggins had been arguing about. Considering Wiggins's penchant for thinking up new regulations and posting them on signs which he promptly nailed up on the nearest piling, it could be almost anything. Pretty soon, she thought with a little chuckle, he'd run out of pilings.

The bell on the door jangled and Lucy looked up. It was Phyllis.

"Mm-mmm, that coffee sure does smell good," she said, dropping her purse and lunch on the counter. "It's sure nice coming in and having the coffee all made. I'm going to get spoiled."

Making the morning pot of coffee had been one of Phyllis's duties before Lucy started working full-time.

"Better not get used to it," said Lucy. "It's just for the summer."

"Famous last words," said Phyllis.

Lucy smiled and answered the phone. It was Howard White, chairman of the board of selectmen.

"Hi, Howard," said Lucy, picturing his sparse white hair and his long, distinguished face. "What can I do for you?"

"Now, Lucy," he began, clearing his throat. "I know that your reporting is usually very reliable, but I noticed an error in last week's paper. It was in your story about the cemetery commission."

"Really?" Lucy was puzzled. The cemetery commission was hardly controversial, and their last meeting had been typically uneventful.

"I believe you quoted Henry Abbott at some length. . . ."

"Well, he is the chairman, isn't he?"

"He *was* chairman." White paused. "He's dead."

"What? He was there. I saw him myself."

"You saw Bill Cranshaw, the new chairman. He took the job after Henry died last month."

"I got his name from the town report," said Lucy, feeling her face redden. "It's only a few months old. I never dreamed . . ."

"It's quite understandable. Henry's death was quite sudden and unexpected. You will write a correction, won't you?"

"Of course."

Lucy hung up the phone and dropped her head on her desk, groaning.

"Correction?" inquired Phyllis.

Lucy nodded.

"Ted won't be happy."

"Don't I know it," said Lucy, recalling the last time she'd had to write a correction. That time she'd misstated a vote of the school board and Tim had insisted she apologize personally to all five board members. She could still taste the crow she'd eaten that day.

The phone rang again and Lucy reached for it.

"It's me," said her best friend, Sue Finch. "Have you got time for coffee today?"

Lucy glanced at the clock. Ted would be in any minute. No point in rushing things, she decided. She'd have plenty of time to write the correction and explain to him later.

"Sure. Meet you at Jake's in five."

Sue was already at the coffee shop when Lucy arrived. Before leaving the office she'd taken a few minutes to write up her idea for the lobster story and had slipped it in Ted's mailbox. Hopefully, he'd be so pleased with her initiative that he'd overlook her correction.

As she approached the table, Sue jumped up. She was so excited, she could hardly sit in her chair.

"Guess what? Sidra's set the date!"

Lucy gave her a quick hug and they both sat down. "A wedding! When is it?"

"August first."

"But that's only five weeks away. . . ."

"I know. I have so much to do," Sue said smugly, tucking her glossy black hair behind one ear. "I hardly know where to begin."

Lucy smiled at her friend. This was the sort of thing she loved. Something to organize. Ever since she'd quit her job at the town's day care center Sue had been at loose ends, with nothing to do except polish her nails, do her hair, and buy new clothes. She looked great, admitted Lucy, noting her black linen shorts and crisp white shirt topped with a straw hat, but the truth was she had too much time on her hands. No wonder she was excited about organizing the wedding, but Lucy wondered if Sidra might have ideas of her own. After all, she was a sophisticated young woman who'd made a life for herself in New York as a producer on the Norah Hemmings daytime TV talk show.

"What about Sidra? What does she want her wedding to be like?"

"She asked me to plan it for her," said Sue, preening. "She can't leave her job, you know, she doesn't want to let Norah down after she's been so nice to her and all."

Lucy nodded. Norah Hemmings had a summer home in Tinker's Cove and took an interest in the town's youngsters, providing scholarships and advice and, in Sidra's case, a job.

"Why the rush?"

"It's her fiancé, Ron. It's something to do with his business."

"What does he do?"

Sue put her hands together and took a deep breath. She was so excited, she was practically bouncing on her seat. "He's a millionaire."

"Really?"

"Yes! You've heard of Secure.net?"

"Uh, no."

"You haven't? It's just the hottest new Internet company since Amazon!"

"And he works for them?"

"No, no. He *is* them. He's the CEO and founder."

"Wow," said Lucy, honestly impressed. "Sidra made quite a catch." She paused. "How old is he?"

"Young. Her age, I think. Maybe a year or two older." Sue raised her arm and waggled her fingers to catch the waitress's attention. "Of course the money is nice, but the really important thing is that Sidra is happy." She looked up at the college girl who was waiting tables. "I'll just have black coffee, please."

"Orange juice for me," said Lucy, who rather thought she'd drunk too much coffee already today.

"What happened with Geoff Rumford?" asked Lucy.

"I think he didn't want to commit, like all these young fellows today. They call it commitment phobia. I think she just got tired of waiting for him to get serious, and when Ron came along, well, it was like a fairy tale. All the best restaurants, opening nights, gala parties. He swept her off her feet!"

"Like Prince Charming," said Lucy as the waitress set down her juice.

"Exactly," said Sue, lifting up her cup. "That's why I want this wedding to be perfect. They're the perfect couple and I want them to have the perfect wedding."

"To a perfect wedding," said Lucy, raising her glass in a mock toast.

They touched their cups.

"It's only going to be a small, simple affair, fifty people tops. But it's going to be beautiful. A sweet, country-style wedding with beautiful flowers, wonderful food. Everything will be exquisite—and you know what?" Sue leaned forward, across the table. "Wouldn't your gazebo be just the perfect place for it?"

Lucy could just picture it. Bill's beautiful gazebo festooned with garlands of flowers, a white carpet laid across the emerald green grass, a cluster of tastefully dressed, attractive guests surrounding a radiant Sidra and her tall, handsome millionaire groom.

"Thanks for asking," gushed Lucy. "It'll be a privilege. My gazebo is your gazebo."

Chapter Three

Lucy was floating along in a pink-tinted fog when she left the coffee shop, dreaming of old lace and roses. Passing the bake shop, she stopped to look at the mock wedding cake, five layers tall and topped with figures of a bride and groom, that had stood there collecting dust ever since she could remember.

She shook her head. Sue would never allow a monstrosity like that at Sidra's wedding. Instead she would have something truly beautiful, perhaps covered with real flowers. And the cake inside wouldn't be that dry, crumbly stuff that tasted of chemicals; it would be buttery and rich and filled with jam. Lucy could picture it—she could almost taste it—when she suddenly remembered Bill.

What had she been thinking? She should never have agreed to let Sue have the wedding in the gazebo without checking with him first. She could just imagine his reaction. He was already upset with her for working full-time; he would no doubt want to know where she was going to find the time. And he was right. Now that she thought about it, really thought about it, she realized she simply didn't have time to plan a wedding.

Ah, but she didn't have to, she reminded herself. She

wasn't planning the wedding. Sue was doing all the work. She was simply letting Sue use the gazebo. What was the problem with that? Come to think of it, Bill ought to be flattered that Sue had asked. Lucy was smiling as she pushed open the door to the *Pennysaver* office.

"Well, don't you look like the cat who ate the canary," said Phyllis by way of greeting. Behind her, the fax machine was humming and spewing out sheets of paper. "Have you got a scoop?"

"I wish," said Lucy, tilting her head at Ted's vacant desk. "Has Ted come in yet?"

"Nope."

Lucy headed for her desk, where she looked up Bill Cranshaw's phone number. She reached for the phone, then stopped. It would be better, she decided, if she wrote the correction before she called. Then she could read it to him and assure him she had taken appropriate action and was setting the record straight. She opened a file and typed a few words, then deleted them. She was just starting over when Phyllis dropped several sheets of paper on her desk.

"Fax for you."

Lucy glanced at it. To her surprise, it was from Sue. Since when had Sue had a fax machine? she wondered as she scanned the neat, round handwriting.

"Re: Wedding," Sue had written in businesslike fashion. "Could you check on these for me?" Below this brief introduction was a list of things to do for the wedding.

"Order porta potties" was at the top of the list.

Trust Sue to think of everything, she thought. Of course, it was a good idea. She suspected their septic system was strained to the limit by the kids' lengthy showers and the endless loads of wash she was always doing. Goodness knows it wouldn't do to have it fail in the middle of an elegant social event like a wedding.

"Grade drive and fill potholes" was next.

Another good idea, she thought. There were an awful lot of potholes, and they certainly weren't doing the car and truck any good. Bill could probably get one of his contractor friends to do it for free.

"Canopy for rain?" was the third item. Lucy chewed her lip. What if it did rain? Not on Sidra's wedding! That would be a tragedy. But if it did, would a canopy be large enough? Maybe they needed a tent. Would that spoil the effect of the outdoor wedding? Maybe they could move the whole thing onto the porch or into the house. She really needed to talk to Sue about this, so she circled the item.

Next, Sue had written "Rent chairs." Good idea, thought Lucy, picturing a few neat rows of white folding chairs. How many would they need, she wondered, putting down a question mark.

"Reserve space at kennel for dog." No argument there, thought Lucy. Eating half a pie was one thing; demolishing an expensive wedding cake was something else entirely. She didn't want to risk it.

"Garden flowers," the next item on Sue's list, gave her pause. What did she mean? Lucy thought ahead to August, when her flower beds were filled with brightly colored zinnias and marigolds and some early chrysanthemums. They were dependable, sturdy plants, but they would hardly do as a backdrop for a wedding.

Lucy shook her head. They'd have to check with a nursery to see what would be available then—and affordable.

"What have you got there?" asked Phyllis, intruding on her thoughts. "You're studying it like it's the Ten Commandments or something."

Lucy chuckled. "It *is* the Ten Commandments according to Sue. Sidra's getting married this August and they want to use my new gazebo."

"Won't that be lovely," cooed Phyllis. A single woman herself, she was unabashedly romantic where others were concerned. "I can just picture it, all covered with flowers. And Sidra. Won't she be a beautiful bride! All in white, surrounded by bridesmaids. Have they chosen the colors yet?"

"I don't think so. I guess that's why Sue wants to know what will be in bloom in my garden. Gosh, I wish I hadn't planted those mixed zinnia seeds. They always give you so much red and orange and hardly any lavender or white."

"They could use peach," said Phyllis, "or a pale yellow."

Lucy considered. "You know what I think would work? Kind of a sagey green, leaf-colored, you know, not mint green."

"Good idea," agreed Phyllis, looking over her shoulder at the list and pointing at the next entry.

"If you spray for bugs, do it the day before so you don't have that chemical smell."

"I never thought of that." Lucy paused, staring at the single word "lawn." Truth be told, they didn't really have a lawn. They had sparse patches of grass, separated by areas of pebbly, hardscrabble soil. By August, Lucy knew the little bit of green they had would be dried and brown.

"Well, this wedding will be a good excuse for sprucing up our yard. It has gotten kind of shabby, especially the lawn. I'll ask Bill to give it some fertilizer and water. That ought to green it up."

"You can fill in with sod at the last minute if you have to," said Phyllis.

"Won't that be expensive?"

Phyllis shrugged. "It is a wedding, after all."

Of course, thought Lucy. It was a wedding. The grass would have to be green.

"Don't forget parking," advised Phyllis. "You'll have to rent a cop."

"Thanks for reminding me," said Lucy, adding it to the list. "We don't want to block Red Top Road."

"No, you don't. My sister had a party last month and

people parked in the road and the cops came and made everybody move their cars. You don't want that."

Just then the door flew open and Ted marched in, his camera bag slung over his shoulder. Phyllis scurried back to her desk and Lucy guiltily stuffed the list in her purse. He glanced at her curiously through his horn-rims.

"Is something going on that I should know about?"

"No," she said, reaching for the phone and dialing Bill Cranshaw's number. He answered after the second ring.

"It's a little late for an apology," he complained, after she'd explained her error. "The ones you really ought to apologize to are Bud Abbott's family. Frankly, I don't know how anybody could have made such a stupid mistake."

Lucy swallowed hard. "Well, I don't ordinarily cover the cemetery commission meetings. I was filling in for Ted—he was away for a few days, or he would have caught my mistake when he edited the story. Like most mistakes, it was a combination of factors."

"Seems to me if your byline is on the story you ought to be sure of your facts."

"You're absolutely right," agreed Lucy, thinking it was about time to wind up this conversation. "In the future I will be sure to do that."

"And I don't know what good a correction will do," continued Cranshaw.

"Well, it will set the record straight," said Lucy, tapping her fingers on the desk.

"Seems to me it will just reopen the whole issue. Might be better to just let sleeping dogs lie."

Lucy took a deep breath. "It's our policy to run corrections when we've made a mistake. It's important for our credibility."

"The best way to improve your credibility would be not to make mistakes in the first place."

"You're absolutely right," said Lucy, repeating herself. "But since we're mortal we do make mistakes. That's why we have the correction policy."

She glanced over at Ted and noticed he was chuckling.

"Where exactly will this correction be printed? On the front page?"

"No-o-o," said Lucy, wondering if Cranshaw had ever read the *Pennysaver*. "On page two, where we always put them."

"I guess that'll be all right, then," he admitted in a grudging tone. "Nobody looks there anyway."

"The correction will run next Thursday," said Lucy. "Good-bye."

At his desk, Ted's shoulders were heaving with laughter.

"What's so funny?" she asked testily. "That guy was impossible. After making all that fuss, he decided he didn't want a correction after all."

"You're a bit touchy today, aren't you? Not everything is about you, you know. I was laughing at this letter complaining about the new harbormaster," he replied. "It describes him as 'grimacing and hopping around like a jumping jack.' "

"That's Wiggins for you," said Lucy, remembering her encounter with him that morning. "He's a weird guy. He's got disgusting habits. That mustache of his is . . ."

"An alien life form," said Phyllis, finishing the sentence for her.

"That's small-town nepotism for you," said Ted. "There's only one reason why he got the job. His uncle and two cousins are on the waterways commission."

"Speaking of the waterfront," began Lucy, sensing an improvement in Ted's attitude toward her, "how about letting me do a story on that lobster research project?"

Ted groaned. "Lucy, you can't even tell the living from the dead! Why do you think you can handle a science story with all that technical jargon?"

"I think I can handle it. Especially since Toby is working on the project."

"So he could explain all the really big words to you?" Ted's mouth was twitching at the corners. This time she was sure he was laughing at her.

"Considering the high cost of a college education today, I sincerely hope so."

Lucy knew she could count on some sympathy from Ted on this point. His own son, Adam, was the same age as Toby and had just completed his freshman year.

"Okay," said Ted. "And while you're down there, it wouldn't hurt to keep an eye on Wiggins." He paused. "So how are those obits going?"

"Not going," admitted Lucy, scrabbling around on her desk for the file folder. "Coming. Right now."

"Good. You know what I always say."

Lucy knew. "More people read the obituaries than any other part of the paper."

Chapter Four

"*Memorial donations may be sent to the Tinker's Cove Fire and Rescue Department,*" typed Lucy, adding the final period with a flourish. It was a nasty job, but somebody had to do it. Now, thank goodness, she was done—for this week, anyway.

A disquieting thought occurred to her. If she'd typed Henry "Bud" Abbott's obituary, why hadn't she remembered it when she wrote the story about the golf commission? A brain freeze? A senior moment?

"Phyllis, tell me the truth," she said. "Am I losing my mind?"

Phyllis looked at her curiously. "You want the truth?"

Lucy thought for a minute. "Yes," she finally said. "It seems to me that I'm awfully forgetful lately. Maybe it's Alzheimer's or something."

"I know the feeling," said Phyllis, taking off her reading glasses and wiping them with a tissue. "The way I see it, there's only so much space in our brains. As we get older, the space fills up. Since there's only a limited amount of room left, we can only remember the really important stuff."

"Like whether or not we need to pick up milk?"

"Right." Phyllis nodded. "Or in my case, where I left my reading glasses."

Lucy chuckled. "Thanks. You've made me feel a lot better." She checked the clock and saw it was almost noon. Lunchtime. And today, she definitely wanted to get out of the office.

"It's such a nice day, I'm going to eat outside," she told Phyllis. "I'll be back by one."

"Enjoy—and don't forget your lunch!"

"Ha, ha," said Lucy, swinging the insulated bag.

Pushing open the door with the little tinkly bell, she blinked at the sudden brightness outside. The sun was so strong that everything seemed to be sparkling; rays of light bounced off the cars parked along Main Street, heat waves rose from the asphalt roadway, and even the concrete sidewalk seemed glaringly white. Window boxes and planters, filled with geraniums by the chamber of commerce, added shimmering dabs of green and red, and the light poles were decorated with red, white, and blue bunting in anticipation of the Fourth of July parade just a week away. The sidewalk was filled with family groups of tourists, pausing here and there in little clusters to examine the goods displayed in shop windows, or studying restaurant menus.

Bill's parents, who had moved to Florida, often complained about the heat there, but to Lucy this unaccustomed blast of heat was welcome. Even in summer, temperatures above eighty degrees were rare in this part of Maine, where ocean breezes had a constant cooling effect. As she walked along, Lucy raised her face to the sun and sniffed the clean, fresh air. With bare arms and sandals on her feet, she felt light and free. Almost like a kid again.

"Beautiful day, isn't it?"

Lucy stopped and smiled at Ralph Winslow, who was standing in the door of his antique shop.

"I wish we could bottle it and save it for January," said Lucy.

"You'd make a fortune," he replied.

Lucy gave him a little wave and turned the corner onto Sea Street. From there she could see the whole harbor studded with the tall masts of sailboats. In general, she noticed, the sailboats and recreational boats were berthed on the right side of the main pier, which was stationary. Floating walkways extended from the pier to provide access to the slips. The bigger commercial fishing boats and the ferry to Quisset Point had the left side, near the boat ramp and the loading dock for the trucks that carried the day's catch to market. Boat owners paid a hefty price to rent a slip, but even so there was always a waiting list. Those not fortunate enough to get a slip anchored their boats at moorings out in the harbor and had to row back and forth from their boats in a dinghy, or what old-timers called a pram.

As she drew closer to the waterfront, Lucy sniffed the mixed scent of creosote and diesel fuel, with a touch of salt and fish, that she had come to love. To her it was the essence of Tinker's Cove, where the ocean wasn't just a playground for vacationers but had provided a livelihood for generations of hardy working folk. It was a risky way of life, and fishermen were finding it increasingly difficult to make a living. Nevertheless, Lucy could understand its appeal. There was a sense of adventure that was part and parcel of every sea voyage, whether it was the ten-minute ferry ride to Quisset Point or a round-the-world cruise.

Taking a seat on a bench, Lucy opened her lunch and took a bite of ham on rye. She rolled up her pants and stretched her legs out, taking her chances with skin cancer in order to get a touch of tan on her winter-white skin, and relaxed. It was peaceful and quiet. From somewhere she heard the distant sound of hammering and the thrum of a motor, gradually becoming louder. She wondered if it might be Geoff and Toby, aboard the

Lady L, but when the boat came in sight it was Chuck Swift's Osprey.

Lucy ate her lunch, watching as Chuck docked and unloaded his catch, neatly packed in plastic boxes. When she'd finished her apple and he was hosing down the deck, she approached him, once again ignoring the sign and keeping an eye out for Wiggins.

"How's the fishing?" she asked when he looked up.

"Can't complain," he said, grinning. "Not on a day like today."

Chuck was a muscular fellow in his late twenties with a ruddy, broad face. He was wearing rubber boots and bright yellow foul-weather pants with suspenders. His stained and worn T-shirt advertised Moat's Boat Yard: MOAT'S: EVERYTHING YOU NEED TO STAY AFLOAT.

"Did you see the Lady L out there?" she asked, shading her eyes with her hand.

"Didn't see 'em but I heard 'em on the radio. They're out by Pogey Point."

Lucy nodded. She knew the fishermen kept in touch by radio, gossiping over the airwaves like housewives used to do on the telephone in the days when women stayed home.

Chuck jumped up onto the dock and hoisted a box full of lobsters. "Got my quota today," he said, referring to a new regulation limiting lobster catches. "But you know, some days I'm still out there at six, seven at night and still not near it."

"They're getting scarce, that's for sure," Lucy said. "Maybe this research project will help. I'm going to write a story about it for the *Pennysaver.*"

He cocked his head. "And you probably want me to say that it'll be the salvation of the industry or some such thing, don't you?"

Lucy raised an eyebrow in surprise. "You don't think it will help?"

"Maybe," said Chuck, dumping the box on the scales and scrawling the weight on the lid. "It seems to me that every time they try to help us they just come up with something that costs us money. Safety equipment, quotas, rules and regulations—it's sure not the business it used to be. My grandfather wouldn't recognize it, that's for sure."

"I suppose not, but you've got to admit that if they can identify this parasite . . ."

"What are they gonna do? Vaccinate all the lobsters?"

"Uh." Lucy was stumped. "You got me there."

"Don't get me wrong," said Chuck. "I'm not against the project; I'm just not getting my hopes up. Like that meeting they're talking about going to, to complain about the new waterways policy. We can go and make a fuss, but you know it's not going to change anything."

"What new policy?" Lucy was definitely interested. Maybe that was what Geoff and Wiggins had been arguing about earlier.

"You know, raising the fees and saving the bigger slips for recreational boats."

Hearing a blast from a ship's horn, Lucy and Chuck looked up to see an enormous, gleaming white yacht gliding into the harbor.

"Wow," said Lucy. "What's that?"

"That is some rich guy's private yacht."

"I never saw anything like that here before."

"Well, you're going to see a lot more of 'em. It's getting too crowded on Nantucket or something, so they're coming our way. And the waterways commission is seeing green. Charging big bucks for prime docking space."

"But where do they put them? There's a waiting list for even a little slip."

"Right you are," agreed Chuck. "But that doesn't matter to the commission. When one of these pleasure palaces arrives, they just move somebody out into the harbor, or make us double up. Kinda like you do with your kids when you've got company."

"But you've paid for your slip . . ."

Chuck shook his head. "Not anymore. We pay for *docking privileges*—not a particular berth."

"But how can you load stuff on and off the boat?"

"You use the dock, and then you move. It's a pain in the chops because when you're all done you're not all done—you've got to move the boat."

"But why don't they keep those big boats out in the harbor?"

Clarence rubbed his thumb against his fingers. "Big bucks. Those babies pay by the foot. Bigger boats get precedence. That's the new policy." He paused. "That one out there, it's seventy feet if it's a yard. Plus, they pay transient rates. The town'll probably get as much from her in a week as they get from me in a season."

Lucy gazed at the sleek yacht, all sparkling white and clean as a new penny. "SEA WITCH, FORT LAUDERDALE" was painted on its stern. It made quite a contrast to the rust-stained, tubby working boats with their cluttered decks full of nets and gear.

"I see," she said. "Well, I'm just a working girl. It's back to the old grind for me."

"Tell me about it," said Chuck, taking hold of a wheelbarrow and pushing it down the dock to retrieve the rest of his catch.

Walking back to the office, Lucy didn't notice the fine weather. She marched along, wondering how it could be that some people had to work their fingers to the bone and risk their lives in order to make a living and others could just sail around in the lap of luxury. And if that wasn't bad enough, here was the town displacing working people in favor of these idlers with well-padded wallets. As if they were some sort of superior beings just because they had lots of money. It just wasn't fair, and she was going to look into it. It was about time the people of Tinker's Cove learned how their prime natural resource, their harbor, was being sold to outsiders.

Sold by the foot, she told herself. Now there was a headline.

Chapter Five

Back at the *Pennysaver*, Lucy yanked the door open and set the little bell jangling.

Phyllis looked up and handed her a pink message slip. Lucy glanced at the notation to "Call Sue" and realized Phyllis hadn't greeted her. Something was up. She cast a questioning glance at Phyllis, who tilted her head in Ted's direction. Lucy got the idea.

"I know I took a long time for lunch, but that's because I was working on a story. Have you heard about this new harbor policy?"

"Were you thinking at all when you wrote these obits?" asked Ted, his voice dripping with sarcasm. "Typos. Lots of typos. According to you, the late Fred Dunmeyer was a *diary* farmer! And then there's Sylvia Appleton, I quote you, "a former school *barbarian!*"

"Okay. Okay." Lucy waved her hand impatiently. "No big deal. Minor details. I'll fix them. Listen to me a minute. This is a major story."

Ted sighed and shook his head. "No, it isn't. We ran it a few weeks ago, when the commission voted."

Lucy was dismayed. "The commissioners decided to displace the working fishermen in favor of rich millionaires with yachts and you don't think it's a big story?"

Ted started to explain, but he was interrupted by Phyllis.

"Millionaires? Where?" she asked.

"At the harbor. You should see the yacht that's just pulled in. Very big. Very white. From Fort Lauderdale."

"Is it anybody famous?"

"That's an idea, Lucy," said Ted. "Why don't you find out who it is. Now that could be a story. Maybe it's a movie star."

Lucy threw her hands up in frustration. "Don't you get it? We have this huge income gap in this country. Five percent of the people have eighty percent of the wealth, leaving twenty percent for the rest of us. And here we have local, hardworking fishermen finding their job is becoming a lot harder because the town is selling their dock space to the highest bidder."

"It's not such a bad idea, Lucy," said Ted, leaning back in his swivel chair. "The harbor's in bad shape. The pilings are rotting away; they need to dredge. All that costs money, and the commission figured this would be preferable to raising the fees for everyone."

"Oh," said Lucy, feeling like a deflated balloon.

"Lucy," began Ted, "I'm curious. Do you ever read the paper?"

"I'm too busy writing it," she snapped. "So, what next? The police log? The real estate transactions?"

"Both." He handed her a thick sheaf of papers.

She groaned.

"And when you're done, find out who's on that yacht."

She flipped through the police log. Extra long, she noticed, probably because school was out. She fingered the pink message slip; better call Sue before she got started.

"It's me. What's up?"

"Guess what?" Sue's voice was breathless with excitement. "Ron and Thelma are in town and I want you to meet them."

Lucy drew a blank. "Who are Ron and Thelma?"

"Sidra's fiancé and his mother."

"Ohhhh," said Lucy. "*That* Ron and Thelma."

"And it's important for you to meet them since the wedding is going to be in your gazebo."

"Okay. Did you have a time in mind?"

"How about this afternoon? We could have tea."

"Four o'clock. Great."

"Four's a little early. Could you make it at five?"

"I have to pick up the kids then."

"Couldn't Bill pick them up, or somebody else?" Lucy could hear the tension in Sue's voice.

"I guess so," she said, unwilling to add to her friend's stress level. She had enough to cope with, planning the wedding.

"Great! See you later!"

"Great," muttered Lucy, hanging up the phone.

Darn. She couldn't call Bill—he had gone to New Hampshire to buy salvaged millwork from an 1800 house that was going to be demolished. Zoe's best friend, Sadie Orenstein, was also at the Friends of Animals day camp; maybe her mother would take the girls home. Geoff Rumford probably wouldn't mind giving Toby a lift, and they could pick up Elizabeth on the way. Give the girl a thrill. She was dialing when she heard Ted's voice.

"You don't seem to have gotten very far on that police log."

"I know. Transportation crisis. Got to get rides for the kids."

"I don't mean to be unsympathetic, but you seem to be spending a lot of time on personal issues. What's with all these messages from Sue? Can't you talk to her on your own time?"

Lucy rolled her eyes. "I got one message."

"So you say." Ted didn't sound convinced.

"But Sidra's getting married, you know."

"That's nice. What's it got to do with you?"

"I'm helping Sue with the wedding."

"Ahhh, so that's it," said Ted, nodding and placing the tips of his fingers together. "I hope that this wedding isn't going to interfere with your work. After all, your job is a lot more important than a wedding."

Lucy couldn't believe what she'd just heard. She looked across the room at Phyllis, who was also equally incredulous. They turned in unison to face Ted.

"Nothing's more important than a wedding," asserted Lucy.

"That's right," chorused Phyllis. "You tell him."

Ted looked at the two women, then blinked and swallowed hard.

"Well, just so you get your work done," he said, retreating to the tiny morgue, where they stored the back issues.

Lucy felt a little thrill of anticipation when she drove the Subaru into Sue's driveway and parked. She was finally going to get a look at Sidra's millionaire fiancé. Her experience with millionaires was limited; the only certified millionaire she knew was Norah Hemmings. Not that she knew the talk show host very well. In fact, Lucy only knew her at all because Norah's son Lance was Elizabeth's on-again, off-again boyfriend. Although Norah was definitely a charismatic person, she didn't really appear wealthy. That was probably part of her appeal, thought Lucy. Millions of middle-class women wouldn't turn on the TV to watch someone they couldn't identify with, someone like those perfectly groomed and coiffed women pictured with their winning horses in *Town & Country* magazine.

As an Internet millionaire, Ron didn't have to worry about offending the viewing public with obvious displays of wealth. He probably looked like the men in Ralph Lauren ads, thought Lucy, or those haughty fellows in the Brooks Brothers ads. They were always tall and tanned and muscular, with sharply defined jaws and straight teeth. Straight hair, too, which the wind blew away from their faces. They were the sort of men who faced the wind and defied the elements, guys who were so sure of themselves that they could dare to wear pink shirts.

Lucy had hardly gotten herself out of the car when the door flew open and Sue ran out to greet her.

"What took you so long?" she demanded, nervously wringing her hands.

"I got here as soon as I could." She gave her friend a quick hug and noticed how tight her shoulders were. "Is something the matter?"

"Oh, no," insisted Sue. "It's just that I've never met them and, well, it's a bit awkward. We don't seem to have much in common."

"Well, they're from New York. It's a different world," said Lucy, giving Sue's hand a squeeze. "Just remember you do have something in common—Sidra. You all love Sidra."

"That's right," said Sue, leading her through the house to the deck overlooking the backyard. Stepping through the sliding doors, Lucy spotted Sue's husband, Sid, standing against the railing. He worked as a finish carpenter and usually wore jeans and work boots, but Sue must have insisted he get home early and change. His hair was still damp from a shower, and he was looking rather uncomfortable in a dress shirt and chinos—he looked as if he had gained a few pounds since he wore them last. Lucy gave him a big smile while she waited to be introduced to the others. Sid nodded solemnly.

"This is my best friend, Lucy Stone," said Sue, draping an arm across Lucy's shoulders. "Lucy, this is Thelma Davitz and her son, Ron."

Lucy had a gracious little speech all prepared, but it

flew out of her mind when she was finally confronted with Ron and Thelma. All she could manage was a little "Hi," delivered in a squeaky voice.

"Lovely to meet you," said Thelma, extending her plump little hand. Her arm was paved with gold bracelets and her fingers were covered with enormous rings.

Lucy gingerly grasped the proffered hand, hoping she wouldn't be injured by a protruding gemstone.

Meeting Thelma's eyes, which were bristling with fake eyelashes, Lucy took in her brittle, bleached hair, her remarkably taut and unlined face, and the numerous chains draped around her crepey neck. Continuing her survey, Lucy noticed the designer warm-up suit Thelma was wearing. It was made of some shiny, silky material that Lucy doubted would actually absorb a single bead of sweat and was trimmed with glittering gold braid. Thelma was wearing matching gold sandals, and her toenails, like her fingernails, were polished with bright-red lacquer.

Turning to greet Ron, Lucy struggled not to show how disappointed she was. Ron was not the groom she had imagined for Sidra; she suspected that if Ron ever ventured into Brooks Brothers or Ralph Lauren he would be politely ushered to a back room. He was tall and dark, all right, but he wasn't handsome. His nose was too big, his chin too small. His shoulders were narrow, and although he was thin, he didn't appear to be in very good shape. His pale white skin, though it would have gladdened the heart of a dermatologist, had the unfortunate effect of emphasizing his five o'clock shadow. Worst of all, he was wearing black socks with shorts and sandals.

"It's so nice to meet you," murmured Lucy, wondering what in the world Sidra saw in this fellow.

He didn't bother to get out of his chair, or even to take her proffered hand. Instead, he raised one hand in a little wave, as if he were making that last half turn to install a new light bulb.

"Congratulations are in order, I think," said Lucy, taking a seat. "You're very fortunate to have won Sidra's heart."

"Uh," he said, peering at her through his thick, black-framed eyeglasses. He blinked. "Thank you," he finally said, as if trying out a new phrase in a foreign language.

Lucy glanced at Sid, wondering what he thought of his future son-in-law. From the way he was glowering, Lucy guessed he wasn't quite ready to welcome him into the family.

"Now what would you all like to drink?" asked Sue. "I have iced tea, beer, wine. What would you all like?"

"I'll have iced chai latte," said Thelma. "So yummy."

"Oh, dear," said Sue. "I don't think I have that. In fact, I don't know what it is."

Thelma looked at her as if she must be a new arrival from Mars. "It's all the rage in New York."

"I'm sure it is," replied Sue. "This is Maine. We're just catching on to iced coffee."

"Well, then, iced tea will be fine."

"Same here," said Ron.

"I'll have wine," said Lucy, pretty sure that Sue was dying for a glass but wouldn't drink unless someone else did.

"A beer for you, Sid?" asked Sue, in a bright tone.

"Sure," he growled back.

Lucy was about to offer to help with the drinks, but she realized her job was to entertain the Davitzes—not to gossip about them in the kitchen.

"Did you have a nice trip?" she asked.

"Marvelous," said Thelma, gesturing with her hands and setting her jewels to twinkling and clinking. "Of course, the yacht is the best way to travel. So roomy and comfortable, and the crew do absolutely everything for you."

Lucy was momentarily speechless. "Ah," she said.

"That was your yacht I saw in the harbor today at lunchtime?"

"Well, the Sea Witch isn't really ours. We're just renting him for the summer."

"*Her*, Mom," corrected Ron in a sharp voice. "You call yachts *her.*"

"Well, how am I supposed to know that?" demanded Thelma. "I come from Englewood, New Jersey."

Hoping to prevent an argument, Lucy posed a question.

"So, Ron," she asked, "how do you like the seafaring life?"

"Oh," he said, pausing to find just the right word, "it's okay."

"He's so modest," said Thelma, somehow managing to include a note of criticism in her compliment. "You'd never know to look at him that he's well on his way to becoming the next Bill Gates."

"Aw, Mom," said Ron, looking down at his feet.

"It's true." Thelma patted her bosom, a gesture that served to emphasize both her jewelry and her ample endowment. "Sidra is one little miss who's doing very well for herself."

Lucy saw Sid's face redden, but he didn't say anything.

Just then Sue returned with a tray of drinks. Her eyes widened in reaction, but she graciously recovered.

"I think they're *both* very lucky. Here's a toast to our wonderful children."

"Here, here," said Lucy, raising her glass.

Thelma also raised her glass and clinked it against Sue's, but Ron didn't seem to notice. He downed his tea in a gulp and sat holding the empty glass.

"Can I get you another?" asked Sue, determined to be the gracious hostess.

"Nah," said Ron, tapping his foot impatiently.

"I think having the wedding up here in Maine is a wonderful idea," said Thelma, taking a ladylike sip of tea. "It's lovely here and so much more private for Ron. Ever since his company began to be so successful he's been a bit of a celebrity, you know."

Lucy glanced at Ron, but he seemed abstracted and lost in thought. Probably advanced computer stuff, she guessed. HTML or HTTP or ISPs and DSNs, whatever those were.

"It's true, you know," continued Thelma. "He gets requests for interviews all the time, but he always turns them down. I don't know why. People want to know about him."

"Gee, Mom," groaned Ron, rolling his eyes.

"That fellow from *CyberWorld* magazine called again. I really think you should talk to him. He's not like the rest, you know. He'll understand all about what the company is doing." She turned to face Lucy and Sue. "Ron says it's just so difficult talking to most interviewers because they don't have the faintest idea what he's talking about. They're not computer savvy, you see, and he has to explain everything." She turned back to Ron. "But you see, you wouldn't have to explain to him. If he works for *CyberWorld* magazine he must know all about computers."

"I'll think about it," said Ron in a firm voice, for the first time giving a hint of the qualities that had made him so successful. "I thought you wanted to talk about the wedding."

"Oh, the wedding," chortled Thelma. "So exciting, isn't it? And using a gazebo—what a lovely idea. Sue told me all about it. I can't wait to see it. And you know, Sue," she said, resting a bejeweled and manicured claw on Sue's arm, "I'll be happy to help with the wedding any way I can."

"Thank you," said Sue, placing her hand on top of Thelma's. "That's so kind of you. I don't know how to thank you."

"You don't have to thank me. It's my pleasure." Thelma beamed at her. "Now, tell me all about your plans so far. But I guess I'm getting ahead of myself. What about a shower? When is that going to be?"

"A shower?" Sue repeated the word, unsure she had heard correctly.

"Of course! Aren't you giving one? For Sidra's friends. So they can give her gifts."

"I can't give a shower."

"Why not?"

"I'm her mother. Relatives don't give showers. Only friends."

"I never heard of such a silly rule," said Thelma. "But if you insist it's so, just ask one of her friends. How about Lucy here?"

On the hot seat, Lucy squirmed. Sue came to her defense.

"I can't do that, either," she said, firmly.

"Why not? Showers are fun, and her friends will want to give gifts. That's why they call it a shower, you know. You can even put little cards from the stores she's registered with in the invitations, so people will know what she wants. She'll be showered with gifts."

"Maybe her friends in New York will give her a shower," said Lucy.

"I'm sure they will," said Thelma. "But what about her Maine friends?"

Sue shook her head and attempted a bright little laugh. "Most of her Maine friends are probably in New York. Believe me, bright kids don't stick around here. They go to college and move on. They don't come back."

"She must have *some* friends here," insisted Thelma.

"There's Molly Thacher," said Lucy, grinning mischievously. "She already has three kids, and I noticed they've added a carport to the trailer."

From his post at the corner of the deck, Sid broke his silence and laughed.

Sue shot him a warning glance and turned to smile

at Thelma. "We'll just have to let you handle the shower when you go back to New York," she said.

"Oh, didn't I tell you?" Thelma clapped her hands together. "We're not going back to the city. We're staying right here until the wedding. Isn't that fabulous?"

"Absolutely fabulous," said Sue, tipping up her glass to get the last of the wine. "Seconds, anyone?"

Chapter Six

Early morning was Lucy's favorite time of day. Then, before Bill and the kids were up, she could enjoy a few moments to herself. Sometimes she'd read the paper with her coffee, other days she was content to sit at the kitchen table watching the birds at the feeder hung from the old apple tree. This morning, goldfinches were breakfasting on the tiny seeds she had put out for them, perching momentarily on the feeder to extract a seed and then flying off in that bobbing way they had. With the bright yellow feathers and black wings they looked quite exotic, as if they'd be more at home in a rain forest than in her Maine backyard.

Lucy was watching, amused, as two males vied for the same perch, when there was a knock at the door. Who could it be this early, she wondered, pulling her robe together over her nightgown and shuffling across the kitchen floor to the door. Pushing the red-checked curtain aside, she was surprised to see Thelma Davitz.

"I know it's a little early," said Thelma when she opened the door, "but I just wanted to get a tiny peek at your gazebo. I hope you don't mind."

Thelma, Lucy saw, was perfectly coiffed, abundantly

bejeweled, and dressed in a beige suit at half past six in the morning.

Seeing her check the clock, Thelma simpered and fluttered her hands. "It is a trifle early, I know, but there's so much to do to plan the wedding. We don't have a moment to waste, do we?"

"I guess not," said Lucy, clutching her bathrobe and wishing she'd bothered to look for the sash when she got up this morning. She heard the hiss and bubble of the coffeepot and asked Thelma if she'd like a cup.

"Oh, no," said Thelma. "I can't touch it. If I did, I'd never sleep. Besides, I have plenty of energy without it."

Lucy didn't have that problem. "If you don't mind, I'll just grab a cup."

"Just bring it along," said Thelma. "Or point me in the right direction. I don't have time to spare this morning."

"Point you where?" Lucy was having trouble concentrating.

"To the gazebo, of course." Thelma was impatiently tapping her foot, shod in a pair of beige stilettos.

"I'd better go with you," said Lucy, giving up the idea of coffee. She had to figure out where Kudo had gotten to. She didn't like to think what might happen if he encountered Thelma alone in the backyard.

Lucy reached for Bill's jacket, which hung on a hook next to the door, and jammed her feet, slippers and all, into a pair of men's sneakers. They were size twelves and could belong to either Bill or Toby. Then, feeling like Ma Clampett, she pushed the screen door open and clomped out onto the porch.

The squeak of the screen door summoned Kudo, who took it to mean that breakfast was being served. He bounded up the porch steps and greeted Thelma by sticking his nose in her crotch. When she squealed in protest, he reared up on his hind legs and placed his forepaws on her chest, greeting her with a dripping tongue and a big, doggy smile.

"Down, Kudo!" yelled Lucy, dragging him off Thelma and shoving him toward the door. She wanted to lock him inside, but he was having none of it. He wasn't interested in going inside if his food bowl wasn't full, so he circled around her and jumped off the porch to the path, where he stationed himself, ready to go where the action was.

"Are you all right?" Lucy asked Thelma.

"Oh, yes," replied Thelma, smoothing her expensive knit jacket. "I just love dogs."

Lucy didn't quite believe her, and she didn't trust Kudo to behave himself, so she took Thelma's elbow as they went down the steps. Keeping a wary eye on the dog, who was loping along beside them, excited to have company for his early morning rambles, Lucy led the way around the house to the gazebo.

"I think it's such a lovely idea, a real country wedding," trilled Thelma, moving with the speed of lightning in her high heels. How did she manage it? wondered Lucy, who was struggling along in the oversized men's shoes.

"Just look at all the grass and trees and stones and things. It's so-o-o country."

"That it is," agreed Lucy, getting a whiff of manure from the field down the road. Why did they have to pick yesterday of all days to spread manure? Why? Maybe Thelma wouldn't notice.

"Do you smell something?" Thelma tilted her head up and sniffed. "Very unusual. Very earthy."

"It'll be gone by the wedding," said Lucy, crossing her fingers. "All you'll smell is flowers."

They rounded the corner of the house, and the gazebo was suddenly visible. Thelma clapped her hands together, setting her bracelets to jangling.

"It's adorable," she cooed.

"I'm so glad you like it," said Lucy, relieved. She

knew how much Sue wanted to have the wedding there and had been fearful Thelma wouldn't approve.

"But so small." She shook her head sadly. "I don't know if it will accommodate all the people we're inviting."

"Well, I think Sue was thinking that the wedding itself would take place in the gazebo, and we'd have a canopy on the lawn for the congregation."

"Even so . . ." began Thelma.

"How many people are you thinking of inviting?" asked Lucy. "Sue said it would be a small wedding."

"Dear Sue." Thelma blinked her eyes, and Lucy wondered exactly how one managed to apply eyeliner so early in the morning. "I don't think she really has any idea how *important* Ron is, or the circles he travels in. I mean, we were really quite comfortable in Englewood. Ron's father—he was a stockbroker, you know—left us very well provided for. But that was nothing to the success Ron's had. Did you see his photo in the *New York Times* last week? He was at that Computers for Kids benefit a few weeks ago at the Met. That's a museum, dear, in New York."

Thelma had seated herself on one of the chairs and had neatly crossed her ankles.

"He was photographed with Barbara Walters, and all these Astors and Vanderbilts were there. It's funny when you think of Ron, the grandson of a pickle manufacturer, hobnobbing with all those people. And do you know what Barbara—that's *Barbara Walters;* I think I mentioned her earlier—well, do you know what she told me? She said that those old fortunes from railroads and oil are just pennies compared to the new fortunes coming from the Internet."

Thelma nodded and paused for breath. Lucy knew she had to act fast.

"Thelma, I really have to get back in the house to wake up the kids. . . ."

"Oh, don't let little me hold you up," said Thelma, jumping to her feet. "I'll just walk back with you, if you don't mind. Just in case the dog comes back."

"That's probably wise," said Lucy, wondering again where Kudo had gotten to.

"You know, dear, I don't like to raise an unpleasant subject, but I couldn't help noticing some doggy poos on the grass."

Lucy was mortified. "Of course, all that will be cleaned up before the wedding."

Thelma was looking around, a little furrow between her brows.

"There don't seem to be very many flowers. I was hoping for apple blossoms and lilacs, you know."

"Well, it's a little late for apple blossoms and lilacs," said Lucy, taking a few steps toward the house in hope that Thelma would follow. "The zinnias and marigolds will be in bloom, and the dahlias. Oh, and the rose of Sharon is beautiful then. And some early mums, of course."

"That does sound nice," said Thelma, who seemed to have rooted herself to the ground. "You know," she continued, "I think it's awfully risky having an outdoor wedding."

"Well, Sue did mention a tent." Lucy paused. "I'm afraid it's getting awfully late. . . ."

"Oh, don't let me hold you up," said Thelma, taking a few baby steps. "What about music? Did Sue mention music?"

"I think she's thought of everything. She even gave me a list, sort of a checklist. . . ."

"Could I see it?"

Lucy's mind was blank. She couldn't remember what she'd done with the list, and she sure didn't have time to look for it now.

"I really have to get the kids up, they're going to be late. . . ."

"I'd really like to go over that list with you."

Lucy was desperate to get rid of Thelma. "I'm sorry," she began, when inspiration struck. "How about lunch?"

"Fortunately, I'm free," said Thelma, implying that this was not usually the case.

"Great. I'll meet you at noon at . . ."

"The Greengage Inn?"

"Fine. I've got to run now," said Lucy, backing off down the path until she reached the corner of the house and then dashing for the porch.

In the kitchen, she was relieved to see that Bill had gotten the kids up, and breakfast, if you counted bologna-on-bagel sandwiches as breakfast, was in progress.

"Who was that woman?" he asked, looking out the window at Thelma. "Is she the Avon lady or something?"

Lucy laughed. "No, no, that's Sidra's mother-in-law to be. The mother of the groom."

"Scary," said Elizabeth.

"Oh, yes," said Lucy, pouring herself that long-delayed cup of coffee.

"What's she doing here?" asked Bill, a puzzled expression on his face.

Lucy didn't think this was the time to explain that the wedding was going to take place in the gazebo.

"She just wanted some information about caterers and florists," she said.

"This early in the morning?"

"Tell me about it," she said, carrying the coffee upstairs to drink while she got dressed. She set the cup on her dresser and opened the closet door, looking for something to wear. She had planned on jeans and a polo shirt, but that wouldn't do at the inn, so she flipped through the hangers looking for something that didn't need to be ironed. She had almost reached the end of the pole when a large box tumbled down from the top shelf.

Reflexively, Lucy put her hand up to protect her

head and was soon smothered in white organza. Stepping back into the room, Lucy freed herself from her wedding dress. Holding it against herself, she turned to look in the full-length mirror. Magically, her bright pink robe and tousled hair disappeared and she was once again the bride who had walked down the aisle on her father's arm to meet Bill at the altar.

She remembered how she and her mother had searched and searched for that dress. They had trudged from one bridal shop to another for weeks before they spotted it, displayed in a second-story window on Lexington Avenue.

"It's perfect," her mother had assured her when she emerged from the dressing room.

And she was right. The dress was just what she had been dreaming of. The bodice and short cap sleeves were made of alençon lace, and the waist was nipped in with a satin sash that topped a full, swirling organza skirt.

Lucy remembered the fittings. How embarrassed she'd felt standing in her underwear while a terrifying seamstress with a mouthful of pins took all her measurements. She'd had to go back several times while the woman clucked over her. Worst of all was standing very still for what seemed like hours as she measured and marked and pinned up the endless yards of skirt and underskirts for hemming.

And then, finally, her wedding day. Her mother and bridesmaids had fussed over her, taking forever to fasten the twenty or more buttons that went up the back. Then, sitting on a white sheet in the backseat of her uncle's Cadillac, she was driven to the church, where the long, white carpet stretched before her. Clutching her father's arm with one hand and her bouquet with the other, she had stood waiting for the organ chords that marked the beginning of Mendelssohn's wedding march.

"Mom! We're gonna be late!"

Sara's voice roused her from her reverie and she quickly replaced the dress in its box. She slid it back on the shelf and grabbed her best pair of khakis.

Lucy was only fifteen minutes late, having disregarded all speed limits and practically tossed the kids from the car at their various destinations, but Ted wasn't amused.

"It's deadline day, you know," he told her.

"I know—I had car trouble," she lied, unwilling to tell him the real reason.

Fortunately, there were no last-minute glitches and the paper was finished well before the noon deadline. To celebrate, Ted treated Lucy and Phyllis to coffee and doughnuts. They were gathered around Phyllis's desk when the bell on the door jangled and they all looked up.

The visitor was a young man in his late twenties. One glance told Lucy he wasn't from anywhere around Tinker's Cove: he had practically shaved his head and was wearing snug black pants and clunky green leather oxfords and had a messenger's bag slung over one shoulder. He advanced, smiling to reveal a row of pointed teeth and a tongue stud.

"I'm looking for the editor," he said.

"That's me," said Ted, putting down his jelly doughnut and brushing his hand against his pants before extending it. "Ted Stillings."

"Andy Dorfman," said the young man, grasping Ted's hand and shaking it energetically. "From *CyberWorld.*"

"Really?" Ted's interest was piqued. Journalists from national publications rarely showed up in Tinker's Cove. "How can I help you?"

"Well, you know Ron Davitz is in town. . . ."

"No, I didn't," said Ted. "In fact, I don't know who the hell he is. Why don't you sit down and have a doughnut and tell me all about it."

"Thanks." Dorfman pulled up a chair and sat down. "I'm surprised you haven't heard of him," he said, taking a big bite of double-chocolate.

"They say he's the next Bill Gates," said Lucy and Phyllis in unison.

"Is this true?"

Dorfman nodded, his mouth too full to answer.

"What's he doing in Tinker's Cove?"

"Getting married," said Dorfman.

Lucy and Phyllis nodded.

"To Sidra Finch," said Lucy, belatedly remembering Ted had assigned her to find out who was on the yacht.

"You know her?" asked Dorfman. "That's why I'm here. I'm trying to get some background on his bride."

"Sidra's marrying the next Bill Gates and you never told me?" demanded Ted, turning on Lucy and Phyllis.

"I told you she was getting married," said Lucy. "And what did you say? 'I hope this wedding isn't going to interfere with your work.' That's exactly what you said, if I remember correctly."

"Exactly," said Phyllis.

Ted ground his teeth. "You left out one important element. The name of the groom."

"I thought you knew," said Lucy.

"Everybody knows," said Phyllis. "He's the guy on the yacht."

Ted gave Lucy an evil glance, and she shrugged her shoulders apologetically.

"So who exactly is this guy on the yacht?" asked Ted, turning to Dorfman.

"Typical Internet millionaire," said Dorfman with a grin. "He's got a company called Secure.net. They've got a way of encrypting communications programs so the information remains confidential. Unlike now, where anything you put out there can pretty much be intercepted. They've got fab technology." He paused to reach for another doughnut. "He's rich already and he's going to make a fortune when the product hits the market next month."

"I don't understand. What does the company do?" Ted was scratching his head.

"They don't actually *do* it yet, but they say they have figured out a way to transmit information on the Internet and keep it confidential at the same time."

"So *CyberWorld* is doing a story about this Davitz?"

"Yeah. A profile. Boy from New Jersey makes good, marries beautiful girl. That's what I need your help for. I can't find out much about Sidra Finch."

"Well, if I were you, I'd go talk to her folks. They live just a couple of blocks from here."

Dorfman took out his notepad. "And what would their name be?"

"Finch, of course," said Ted, prompting disapproving glares from Lucy and Phyllis.

"Oh," said Dorfman. He sensed he wasn't going to get any more information; Lucy and Phyllis had fallen silent. "Well, thanks for everything," he said, getting up and slinging his bag over his shoulder. "I'm staying in town for a few days. If you want to reach me, I'm at the Queen Victoria Inn."

"Right," said Ted, smiling affably.

As soon as Dorfman had gone, Lucy pounced. "You shouldn't have done that. Now he'll go and bother Sue and Sid."

"This man's a colleague. It's professional courtesy." Ted leaned back in his chair and scratched his chin thoughtfully. "You know, Lucy. You owe me a story. It's too late now, but we can run it next week."

"I'll get right on it," said Lucy. "But to tell the truth, I'm not really sure what this Internet is. I mean, I know what it is, but I don't see how people make money from it."

"Me, either," said Phyllis. "That NASDAQ keeps

going up, and people are getting rich, but the companies don't make any profit. I don't get it."

"Maybe it's time we figured it out," said Ted.

"I'll do my best," promised Lucy. "In fact, I can start right away because I'm going to have lunch with the next Bill Gates's mother!"

Chapter Seven

Lucy was a few minutes late when she arrived at the Greengage Inn—these days it seemed as if she was always late—but there was no sign of Thelma in the charmingly understated dining room with its glazed ochre walls and linen-covered tables. Sue, however, was sitting at a corner table, staring at the clear glass vase that contained a single orange flower.

"You're meeting Thelma?" asked Lucy.

"Who else?" replied Sue with a sigh. "What kind of flower is this?"

Lucy looked at it and shrugged.

"Never saw one before. Why?"

"Just curious," Sue replied in a monotone.

Lucy sat down next to Sue and leaned close. "Everything okay?"

Sue looked directly at her. "What do you think?"

Lucy would have loved nothing more than to verbally rip Thelma to shreds, and she was dying to discuss what Sidra could possibly see in Ron, but she hesitated, sensing that Sue would feel she had to defend her daughter's choice.

"Sid's really behaving like the classic father of the bride," she finally said.

Sue was just starting to answer when Thelma arrived.

"Yoo-hoo," she yodeled from across the room, turning a few heads. Lucy thought it was probably the first time anyone had yodeled in the Greengage Inn.

Waving to Sue and Lucy, Thelma tottered across the room on a pair of ridiculously high-heeled sandals and plopped gracelessly onto a chair.

"Whew!" she exclaimed in a shrill voice. "All the fashion magazines rave about these Manooloo Blahnik shoes, but I gotta tell you they're hell on your feet, especially if you've got a few corns."

"Beauty knows no pain," said Lucy, repeating a favorite expression of her mother's and happily wiggling her toes in her comfy boat shoes.

"It's difficult to be fashionable in Maine," said Sue, perking up a little as she talked about her favorite topic. "High heels are risky because you can't be sure there's a sidewalk. Besides, people don't really dress here. I mean, look at this crowd."

Lucy glanced around the room, which was filled with women dressed in clothing from the better sportswear racks. Thelma was the only one in a designer suit and heels—and the only one who was carrying this year's fashion rage: a large leopard-skin purse.

"Can I get you ladies something to drink?" asked the waitress.

"I guess we don't really need to wait for Corney," said Thelma, unfolding her napkin. "I'll have an iced . . . tea."

After Sue and Lucy had also ordered iced tea, Sue turned to Thelma. "Did you say Corney is coming? Corney Clark?"

"You know her?" Thelma raised her eyebrows.

"Of course. But we hadn't discussed hiring a caterer."

"Oh," said Thelma, pausing to unfold her napkin. "I just thought it would be a good idea to explore all the possibilities."

"What possibilities?" demanded Sue, her voice rising

a notch. "This is going to be a simple wedding in a gazebo, with simple homemade refreshments. The big question is whether we use whole wheat or white bread for the cucumber sandwiches."

"Half and half, I think," volunteered Lucy.

"That is *such* a good idea," trilled Thelma. "But, you know, I do think we could be a little more adventurous. Especially when you think of the sort of people who will be coming."

"Just family and friends . . ."

"I don't think you quite realize how important my son is," said Thelma, eyes flashing. "He can't sneak off and get married in some dark corner, now, can he? Surely you haven't forgotten Norah Hemmings, and there'll be lots of other important people, too. Ron knows so many highly successful people—the sort of people you read about in the columns. They're used to a certain style, a certain standard of entertainment. That's why I have to tell you the gazebo just won't do."

Lucy and Sue were too stunned to reply; they sat dumbly as Thelma took a sip of tea, grimaced, and added several packets of sugar-free sweetener. Then, spotting Corney across the room, she began waving.

"Over here," she shrieked.

Corney hurried across the room and took the empty chair. "Hi, girls," she said in greeting, neatly propping her portfolio against the table leg. Then, reaching across the table, she took Sue's hand and made eye contact. "I am so happy for you," she said in a professionally sincere voice.

Lucy wanted to roll her eyes but didn't. Instead, she looked down at her plate. She was thinking that, in other circumstances, she and Sue would have thought Thelma and Corney were hilariously pretentious, but today they didn't have that luxury. Today they had to take them seriously.

"Thank you," said Sue in her polite voice.

"Isn't this exciting?" Corney demanded, hunching

up her shoulders and hugging herself. "Sidra's wedding! Why, I remember when she was just a little girl." She paused and switched gears, becoming serious. "I want you all to know that I will do my very best to make this the event you've been dreaming of. That is my pledge to you."

Lucy raised an eyebrow. It seemed as if Thelma had already hired Corney.

"I'm puzzled—" began Sue, but she was cut off by Thelma.

"Corney, I just want you to know that money is no object. My son has given me a blank check. 'Mom,' he said, 'I know how much this means to you, and whatever it costs is fine with me.' "

This lofty sentiment, so touchingly expressed, brought tears to Corney's eyes. Rendered momentarily speechless, she clasped Thelma's hand.

"Sid and I are fully prepared—" began Sue, only to be interrupted by Corney.

"I see doves," she said, looking at the ceiling and gesturing with her hands. "A sea of fluttering white wings, released just as the happy couple depart in . . . *a silver hot-air balloon!*"

"Wouldn't that be lovely?" cooed Thelma.

"I don't know . . ." began Sue, doubtfully.

"We can time it so they leave at dusk, and as the balloon disappears into the distance we light up the sky with . . . *fireworks!*"

"Ohhhh," sighed Thelma, in bliss.

"There'll be music, of course—a music and light show. I know just the people. And then, when the fireworks are over, we'll have the orchestra stay so people can dance."

Sue cleared her throat and placed her hands firmly on the table. "I don't—" she began.

"Are you ladies ready to order?" asked the waitress.

"I think we are," exclaimed Thelma. "Now don't be shy. Have whatever you want. This lunch is on me."

Figuring they would share the check, Lucy had decided to have the cheapest thing on the menu, but now she changed her mind. "I'll have a lobster roll," she said.

"The seafood pasta," said Sue, apparently feeling an unusual need for something sustaining.

"Shrimp cocktail for me," said Corney. "I'm on that protein diet."

Thelma ordered lobster ravioli for herself. Glancing at the menu, Lucy wondered what could possibly justify the price.

"I've promised myself that while I'm in Maine, I'm going to eat as much lobster as I can," said Thelma. "It's so delicious."

"We could serve lobster at the wedding," suggested Corney.

"What a good idea!" Thelma was nodding approval, but an expression of annoyance had replaced her smile. "You know, these lobsters are good to eat but they create a lot of mess, don't they? I mean, those traps are piled up all over the place, even in people's front yards! And it's worse down at the harbor. There you get the smell. When the wind's blowing in a certain direction, you can't escape it."

Lucy and Sue exchanged glances.

"And the noise! They come and go at all hours, with no regard for people's sleep. They woke me up this morning when it was still dark! Clattering up and down the dock and yelling and starting motors and I don't know what all. Who would ever think that catching a few lobsters would require so much noise?"

Thelma looked up as the waitress reappeared, carrying a tray. As soon as the plate was set in front of her, she dived in and speared a ravioli with her fork. She popped a few more of them in her mouth while the others were being served, then checked her watch.

"I hadn't realized it was so late!"

Corney consulted her watch. "You're right. We've got to go."

"I hate to pull you away from your lunch."

"Not at all," said Corney. "I'll nibble on something later. Believe me, I've dealt with these people before and they have a little bit of an attitude. They don't rent the mansion and garden to just anyone, you know, so we'd better do our best to make a good impression."

"Mansion?" inquired Sue.

"Just an idea, dear," said Thelma, rising.

"The Hadwen House," said Corney, referring to a luxurious private home that was occasionally leased for weddings. "I mean, I'm not promising, but wouldn't it be great if we could get it?"

Before Sue could frame an answer, the two were gone. Left alone at the table, Lucy and Sue stared at Thelma's and Corney's hardly touched meals.

"I'm a victim of my class," confessed Lucy. "I couldn't do that. I couldn't waste food like that."

"Me either," agreed Sue. "I grew up hearing about the starving Chinese."

"I always volunteered to send them my lima beans, but my mother wouldn't let me."

Lucy was relieved when Sue smiled.

"Mine either." Sue sighed, and took a bite of pasta. "That Thelma is something, isn't she? She's hijacking the wedding."

"What are you going to do?"

"I'll assert my rights as mother of the bride," said Sue. "The bride's parents give the wedding. Everybody knows that. It's custom. I don't think she can just take it away from me. Can she?"

"I think she has."

"Maybe I can take legal action. Get a cease-and-desist order or something."

"Before you do that, maybe you should talk to Sidra. She'd be horrified if she knew what Thelma is planning."

Sue put down her fork. "I'd like to think so, but I'm not sure."

"What do you mean?"

"Well, lately I've had a terrible time getting ahold of her on the phone. She's always out and if I call her at work she's too busy to talk. We haven't had a real conversation in a long time."

"But I thought she wanted you to plan the wedding."

"That's what she said."

"Well, she certainly knows what sort of wedding you'd give. I don't think she's expecting fireworks and doves and hot-air balloons!"

"You're right, Lucy." Sue seemed to brighten at the thought.

"Why don't you pay her a visit? Then you could present a united front to Thelma. Maybe Sidra could get Ron to call his mother off."

"I'd love to go to New York." Sue's tone was wistful.

"Well, what's stopping you?"

Sue lifted her glass and took a long drink of tea before she answered. "Sid."

"Sid won't let you go?"

"It's not that." She paused. "I don't dare leave him here alone."

"He can take care of himself for a few days."

Sue shook her head. "You don't understand. I'm afraid he'll . . . Sid really hates Ron. You should have heard him last night. He went on and on." Sue lowered her voice and imitated her husband's growl. " 'That Ron's not good enough for Sidra. He doesn't look like he's done an honest day's work in his life. Wouldn't know the business end of a hammer from the handle. Couldn't hit a nail on the head if he tried, which he wouldn't because he's too damn lazy.' Not to mention he didn't much like the way Ron criticized his mother."

"He picked up on that?"

"Oh, yes. 'That fella has no respect at all for his mother, talking to her in that tone of voice. Makes you wonder how he'll treat Sidra. I tell you, Sue, if I hear him talking like that to my little girl, I can't guarantee I won't tan his pale, sickly hide for him. That boy could use a tanning.' "

Sue had a flair for mimicry and Lucy couldn't help smiling despite herself.

"What are you grinning at?" Sue glared at Lucy. "It's not funny. I can't leave him here alone. I have to keep an eye on him. God knows what he might do."

"I think you're overreacting. All fathers are like that when their daughters get married. He'll get used to the idea, eventually."

"That's what I'm hoping, but in the meantime, I'm not letting him out of my sight. How am I going to explain to Sidra that her father won't be able to give her away because he's in jail for assaulting the groom?"

"You're being ridiculous. Besides, you can't watch him every minute."

"I know. That's why I hid the gun. Not that I think he'd actually use it on Ron, but I'm not taking any chances. I found it in his bottom drawer but I put it in his winter boots. He'll never find it there." Sue seemed quite proud of the neat way she'd handled this problem.

Lucy furrowed her brow. "I didn't know you had a gun in the house."

"We didn't. It's new—still in the box. I found it when I was cleaning out his dresser this morning."

Lucy was horrified. "He bought a gun and he didn't tell you?"

Sue shrugged. "Of course not, Lucy. He knows I don't like guns. He's hiding it from me, just like he hides his dirty magazines."

Lucy wasn't convinced. "Maybe you should talk with somebody about this. A psychiatrist or something. This doesn't sound like Sid." Lucy paused. "Why would he even buy a gun?"

"Oh, you know men and their toys. He's like a little

kid. Always bringing stuff home and hiding it because he thinks I won't approve. Remember that motorcycle he had a few years ago? Trust me. I've got it under control."

"Yeah . . . and denial is a river in Egypt," muttered Lucy, as the waitress approached them.

"Can I take your plates?" she asked.

"Please."

"Are you ladies interested in dessert today?"

Lucy and Sue both shook their heads.

"Then I'll be back in a minute with the check."

"I think one of the women who left covered it," said Sue.

"Oh, no," said the waitress, hoisting the tray to her shoulder and taking it away.

Lucy and Sue burst into giggles.

"Mrs. Gotrocks. . . ."

"Skipped out on the check!"

Sue reached for her purse. "This one's on me."

"We'll split it," protested Lucy.

"No," said Sue, digging deep into her bag. "I've got it."

Lucy watched while Sue pawed through her purse, finally coming up empty.

"I changed purses this morning. I must have forgotten my wallet."

"Never mind," said Lucy, pulling out her charge card and trying hard not to think of the balance owed. "This one's on me—but it's the last time I go out to lunch with a millionaire's mother!"

Chapter Eight

Wednesday afternoon, when the deadline was past and it was too early to start on next week's issue, was the day Lucy liked to do her big grocery shopping and catch up on her errands. So, after leaving the Greengage Inn, she headed for the IGA. First, however, she had to cash a check at the drive-through.

As she sat in line in her car waiting for a woman in a huge SUV with New Jersey plates to finish her transaction, her mind went back to the lunch. A glance at her checkbook's shrinking balance, and an uneasy awareness of her Visa account's ever-growing balance, made her regret taking the check. Over a hundred dollars for lunch! How was she going to explain this to Bill when he saw the statement?

She had acted on impulse, hoping to lighten some of Sue's burden. Poor Sue certainly had her hands full, she thought. As if coping with Thelma weren't enough, now Sid had to start behaving strangely. What was he doing with a gun? And why hadn't Sue confronted him and asked him about it? It certainly wasn't good for couples to keep secrets from one another, she thought, vowing to tell Bill that the wedding would be in the gazebo. She amended the thought: *might* be in the gazebo.

The large SUV finally moved on and Lucy pulled up to the window.

Back at the house, Lucy spent the next half hour or so unloading the car and putting the groceries away. When she'd finished, she grabbed a peach and the copy of *CyberWorld* magazine she'd picked up at the checkout counter and headed for the gazebo. Kudo trotted along beside her; in his mind any change of location required an escort. When she stretched out on the chaise longue, he took up his usual sentry position on the top step.

Lucy took a bite of peach, caught the juice with the back of her hand before it dripped down her chin, and opened the magazine. She hoped to learn about this new economy everybody was talking about. She flipped past the ads, which were mostly for computers and companies she had never heard of, and started reading a story about the "Hundred Hottest Start-Ups."

Previously she'd thought of Internet companies in terms of retail sales. Nowadays, instead of filling out an order form and sending a check when you ordered from a catalog, you could place your order with the computer. It had made shopping a lot easier—especially if you needed something in a hurry, like Mother's Day flowers for your mother-in-law.

To Lucy's surprise, however, most of the companies in the article didn't sell products—they sold know-how to other companies. They maximized and utilized; they generated and organized; they managed and prioritized; and they all guaranteed results. And right up there in the top fifty was Ron Davitz's company, Secure.net. Lucy read the description, but the only part of it she understood was the thumbnail-sized photo of a smiling Ron. He looked better in miniature, she thought.

He was also, she learned, soon going to become a lot richer than he already was. Analysts agreed the stock would soar to stratospheric heights when the promised software hit the market. As founder of the company, Ron would reap enormous rewards.

Lucy let the magazine drop to her lap and looked up at the roof of the gazebo, where Bill had cut the boards so they all radiated out from a center point. It had been a labor of love that had taken him hours, and it hadn't netted him a cent. As she studied Bill's handiwork, she wondered if Ron had felt the same sense of purpose when he created Secure.net, the same sense of satisfaction when all the pieces came together just right.

It was four-thirty when Lucy awoke with a start. Leaping over the startled dog, she ran to the house and splashed water on her face, combed her hair, and grabbed her purse. It was time to pick up the kids.

First stop was the day camp, where the girls were part of a group of kids waiting for their rides. Sara and Zoe were cheerful and relaxed as they scampered into the car; Lucy noticed they had each gotten a little sun on their faces.

"You better wear sunscreen tomorrow," she told them at the same time she was thinking how healthy that little touch of sunburn made them look.

At the Queen Vic Inn, Elizabeth was waiting for her on the porch. From her sullen expression, Lucy didn't think the day had gone well.

"Tough day?" she asked as Elizabeth took the front seat beside her.

Elizabeth grunted.

"Want to talk about it?" Lucy asked dutifully.

Elizabeth rolled her eyes. "Mrs. McNaughton was all over me today. Said I wasn't working fast enough. I'm only supposed to take twenty-five minutes per room, but I don't see how I can do it that fast. I have to change the sheets, dust and vacuum, clean the bathroom, give them fresh towels—and some of these people are pigs.

One couple left a slice of pizza on the rug—cheese side down! And there's this guy who's got all sorts of papers and a computer and a fax and doesn't want me to touch anything, and then there's the people who put 'Do Not Disturb' signs on their doors all the time. When am I supposed to clean their rooms?"

Lucy was tempted to mention the present state of Elizabeth's room, where so many dirty clothes were strewn on the floor that it was impossible to vacuum, but she bit her tongue. Instead she said, "It's always hard to get used to a new job."

"Now I know how it feels to be a slave," said Elizabeth.

Again Lucy bit her tongue.

"Give it a chance," she said. "You really need the money for college."

"It's just so unfair. Toby gets to mess around on a boat all day and I have to clean disgusting toilets." She shuddered.

As soon as Lucy turned into the parking lot at the harbor, she realized something was up. A group of fishermen had gathered by the harbormaster's shack, and from their attitudes Lucy understood that they weren't there for a friendly chat. She automatically reached for her notebook and camera.

"Can we go on the swings?" asked Zoe.

Hearing the men's raised voices, Lucy came to a quick decision. "No, you better stay in the car." Seeing Elizabeth reaching for the door handle, she added, "You, too, Elizabeth."

"What is this? Now I'm a prisoner? Why can't I come, too?"

Lucy didn't have time to argue. "Later," she said, hurrying across the parking lot.

When she reached the harbormaster's shack, she saw Wiggins leaning in the doorway, smoking a cigarette. Considering the group's collective anger, his casual attitude seemed out of place.

"You can't do this to me," Geoff was complaining. "A mooring won't work. I've got too much equipment to load and unload."

"That's right," agreed one of the others. "Whose harbor is this, anyway? Does it belong to us, who live and work here, or some rich guy?"

This last was met with enthusiastic agreement from the others.

It was then Lucy noticed Ron Davitz, who was standing next to Geoff but a few feet away, as if keeping a safe distance from the fishermen. He looked out of place at the harbor, thought Lucy, noticing how white his skin was—especially his legs, which were well covered with dark hair. His shorts were too short, and he was again wearing black socks with his sandals.

Wiggins cocked an eyebrow at him and flicked his ashes on the ground.

"Try to look at it from my point of view," said Davitz. "People are constantly coming and going at all hours; there's engines and yelling and banging; and if that isn't bad enough, I tell you the stench from . . . something . . . was absolutely unbearable this morning."

"Lobster bait," said one of the men, prompting chuckles all around.

Davitz didn't see the humor. His voice rose. "In case you've forgotten, I'm paying top dollar, and my mother is not comfortable."

Again the men laughed, and Lucy definitely heard someone say "Mama's boy."

"Well, maybe you shouldn't have brought your fancy yacht to a working port," said Chuck Swift, grasping the brim of his long-billed cap and pulling it down.

Ron squinted in the bright sunlight and turned to face Wiggins. "I'm going to say this one more time: My mother was up all night because of the noise. Now what are you going to do about it?"

"There's nothing he can do," said Geoff. "It's the nature of the business. Fishing is noisy, smelly, messy work!"

"I'll handle this," said Wiggins, addressing Geoff. "I'm the harbormaster here and I don't need you to do my business."

"Well, do your job then," said a fisherman Lucy didn't recognize, "and tell this guy that he picked the wrong port. Tinker's Cove is a working harbor. We were here first, and if he doesn't like it he can leave."

"Why can't *you* leave?" countered Davitz. "It's a big ocean. Can't you fish somewhere else?"

The men glared at him, and Lucy thought it was just a matter of time before someone punched him. She was relieved when Geoff broke the tension.

"This is a fishing port," he said. "It was built by and for fishermen. They've fished out of here their whole lives, and their fathers and their grandfathers before them. That's the way it is and that's the way it's going to stay."

Unfortunately, Geoff's little speech had the effect of a rallying cry. The men became more agitated, voicing agreement and moving restlessly.

"Calm down, fellas," said Wiggins, tossing his cigarette butt in the water. "Nobody's saying you have to leave; you just have to use a mooring for the duration." He nodded toward Davitz's yacht.

"I think I speak for a lot of us when I say I don't mind using a mooring, but you've got to let me load and unload off the dock—it's that simple," said Geoff, offering a compromise. "There's too much risk of dropping something overboard from the pram."

Lucy was relieved to see the fishermen nodding agreement. It seemed as if the tension was defusing. Then Ron spoke up.

"What's the problem? It's fishing equipment. It's supposed to get wet, isn't it?"

Geoff turned to face him. "It's not fishing equipment I'm talking about; it's specimen vials and microscopes and tanks. . . ." He clenched his fists and Lucy held her breath, certain his anger was going to get the best of him. His right arm drew back, but he suddenly checked himself and threw his hands up in frustration. "Anything happens to my equipment, Wiggins, and I'm presenting a bill to the town."

He stalked off, and Chuck quickly spoke up. "There's a waterways commission meeting next week . . ."

The men laughed hearing this, and Wiggins gave a little smirk.

"Well, if the commission won't help us out, we'll take it to the selectmen!"

"That's not a bad idea," admitted one of the men.

"We gotta get organized, present a united front," suggested another.

"Say we meet at the Bilge in half an hour?"

At this, the group began to disperse.

Lucy approached Wiggins, hoping to get his reaction to the situation, but he retreated inside the shack and pulled down the window shades. Real professional, she thought, and she hurried after Geoff, catching up to him just as he was preparing to push off in his dinghy.

"Where's Toby?" she asked. It was low tide and she was looking down at him from the dock.

Geoff pointed out to the center of the harbor, where the Lady L was anchored. "He's still on the boat, and he's going to be there awhile longer, since now I have to use the dinghy to unload the boat. I guess Davitz has to have the whole damn dock, all the time."

"Is that what this is all about? Nobody can use the dock?"

"Only Davitz. He's rented the whole thing. So his mother won't be disturbed." He paused, watching as Davitz stumbled awkwardly on the yacht's gangplank. "I'll be damned if I can figure out what she sees in him."

"Me either," agreed Lucy. "But if we knew what makes people fall in love, well, we could sell it and we'd be a lot richer than Ron there."

Geoff managed to produce a grim little smile. "Don't wait; I'll give Toby a ride home," he said, dipping the oars into the water and starting to row.

Lucy stood for a moment watching, lost in thought. She wondered if Davitz realized how foolish he was being. The fishermen might be laughing at him now, but it wouldn't take much to provoke violence. It had happened before over matters that seemed trivial to outsiders. Cutting another lobsterman's lines or poaching his traps could get a person killed.

"Pretty dishy," said Elizabeth, joining her mother and giving Geoff a little wave.

He grinned and raised an oar to her.

"What?" Lucy asked.

"Admit it, Mom. You were looking at Geoff and I don't blame you. He's really good-looking."

It was true, thought Lucy. The sun had streaked his hair and tanned his skin; he rowed easily with well-practiced strokes, moving the little boat quickly across the harbor.

"He reminds me of your father," said Lucy with a smug little smile.

"Gee, he doesn't remind me of Dad at all," countered Elizabeth.

"He should; he's too old for you," said Lucy, reaching for the car door. "Besides, what about Lance?"

Elizabeth had been friends with Norah Hemmings's son for a number of years, ever since he spent a year at Tinker's Cove High School before going off to a private prep school. This summer he was spending part of his vacation touring Europe, before starting college in the fall.

"He's so immature," said Elizabeth, fastening her seat belt. "And besides, he's hardly ever here."

"I bet he'll be here for the wedding," said Lucy, starting the car. "Norah's supposed to come."

"Oh, Mom," protested Elizabeth, "that's weeks away. I can't waste the whole summer waiting for him."

* * *

It was later that evening when the phone rang. To Lucy's surprise, since the kids usually monopolized the phone, it was for her.

"Lucy, I just can't take it," hissed Sue.

"What's the matter?" Lucy was all ears.

"I can't talk now," whispered Sue. "Meet me for coffee tomorrow?"

"Sure," said Lucy, wondering why Sue suddenly felt she couldn't talk on the phone. There was nobody in the house besides her and Sid.

"Eight too early? At Jake's?"

"See you then."

Lucy replaced the receiver and went back to her book, but although her eyes followed the printed words automatically, she wasn't getting their meaning. She was too busy worrying about her friend.

Chapter Nine

Jake's Donut Shack was a beehive of activity every morning; it was where a good portion of the town's working population got fueled up for the day. At Jake's the gossip flowed as freely as the coffee, which was constantly, because Jake promised a "bottomless" cup.

When Lucy entered by the front door, she was hit by a wall of noise coming from the counter, which was packed, and by the almost irresistible aroma of bacon, coffee and fresh doughnuts. She stiffened her resolve to limit herself to a cup of black coffee, reminding herself that she had already eaten her usual bowl of raisin bran, and headed for the tables at the back, where it was quieter.

There she spotted Sue, sitting in a corner. Even from across the room she looked glum, slumped over a newspaper. Lucy touched her on the shoulder and she gave a little jump.

"Wow, you're really tense," said Lucy. She doubted that all this anxiety was caused by the wedding arrangements; something else was going on and she wanted to know what it was.

"I was reading the paper and you startled me," said Sue.

Lucy thought her tone was a bit defensive and re-solved to proceed carefully.

"Something interesting?"

Sue shook her head and shoved the paper aside. "What will you have?" she asked, signaling the waitress.

"Just coffee," said Lucy, feeling rather virtuous.

"Make that two," Sue told Helen, the waitress who had worked at Jake's for as long as anybody could re-member.

"You're making a mistake," said Helen. "We've got French toast on special today. Dollar ninety-nine."

"That's so tempting," said Lucy with a sigh. "But I can't. I really can't."

"How about you?" Helen turned to Sue. "Something sweet might cheer you up."

"I don't think French toast will do it," muttered Sue.

"Oh, dear," said Helen. "This sounds serious. I'll have that coffee in a jiffy."

"You know what I'd like to do?" Sue narrowed her eyes. "I'd like to put Thelma on a griddle, just like a piece of French toast, and watch her sizzle."

Lucy looked over Sue's shoulder to the front of the shop, where the grill and coffee urns were located. She could just imagine Thelma writhing on the grill, her feet in the air, frantically waving her ridiculous shoes.

"What has she done now?" she asked.

Sue pressed her lips together and hissed a reply. "She's throwing a shower."

Lucy looked up as Helen placed two steaming mugs on the table. "But you told her a shower is out of the question. Besides, who's she going to invite?"

"Lucy, do you see a pattern here? No matter what I say, she goes right ahead and does what she wants. In fact, she's already done it. The invitations are in the mail, she said."

"To who?"

"The woman is scary. The CIA could use her. She got hold of Sidra's high school yearbook and got busy on the Internet. She also called Norah Hemmings and got the names of some of her friends at work. All told, she turned up fifty of Sidra's closest friends."

"Wow." Lucy had to admit she was impressed. "I don't *know* fifty people. At least, not fifty people I'd like be in the same room with."

"Neither does Sidra," said Sue. "This is going to be really awkward. I've seen the guest list, and she hasn't seen some of these people in years."

Lucy took a swallow of coffee. "Where's this shindig going to be?"

"On the yacht. Next week."

"She doesn't waste time, does she?"

"There's no moss on that one." Sue drummed her polished fingernails on the table. "I'd like to kill her."

"No jury would convict you," said Lucy sympathetically.

"I've looked forward to Sidra's wedding ever since she was born, you know. I always imagined planning the wedding with her, doing it together. I thought it would be the happiest day of my life. But now, Thelma's just ruined it. She's taken it all away from me. It's going to be everything I hate: pretentious and extravagant and vulgar and horrible. I can't stand it."

"You know what I keep wondering?" asked Lucy, remembering Ron's performance at the harbor the day before. "Has Sidra ever told you why she wants to marry Ron?" She shrugged her shoulders. "Somehow, he doesn't seem like her type, if you know what I mean."

Sue threw up her hands. "That's what Sid keeps saying. Over and over. But I can't go there. Sidra says she wants to marry Ron. She's a big girl now and she can make up her own mind. I'm not going to try to come between her and the man she's chosen. I won't do that. I love her too much to risk losing her."

Since Sue had brought up the subject, Lucy thought she could safely inquire about Sid.

"How is Sid?" She lowered her voice. "Has he noticed that his gun is missing?"

"If he has, he hasn't said anything." Sue looked away, then changed the subject. "I really wanted to have the wedding in your gazebo, but I don't think it's going to happen. They got the Hadwen House."

"I understand. You're dealing with forces beyond your control." Lucy paused, then decided two could play this game. If Sue could change the subject, she could change it back. "It must be weird, having this big secret between you and Sid. He buys a gun and doesn't tell you; you find it and hide it and don't tell him. Isn't it kind of strange?"

Sue's face was set. "It just seems the best way of handling things right now."

Lucy didn't like the sound of this. "You're not afraid of him, are you?" she asked.

Sue's hand jumped and she knocked over her coffee.

"Gee, Lucy. What kind of question is that? Now look what you've made me do!"

Lucy started pulling napkins out of the dispenser and mopping up the spilled liquid.

"It's just a little spill; we can clean it up." Lucy decided she'd gone this far; she might as well go all the way. "I'm worried you might be in an unsafe situation."

"From Sid?" Sue's voice rose, ending with a nervous little laugh. "Don't be silly."

"I'm not being silly. I'm worried about you. You're a nervous wreck, you're whispering on the telephone, and then there's the fact that your husband is building an arsenal."

Sue's jaw was set. "I think you've misunderstood. Things are fine between me and Sid. The only thing I'm worried about is this wedding."

"Speak of the devil," said Lucy. "Ron's just come in." She watched as he made his way past the crowd at the counter and sat down at the first empty table.

Ron had barely settled himself when Lucy's attention was caught by two very muscular young men who had taken the table adjacent to Ron's. They were dressed in casual clothes, but something about their attitude wasn't casual at all. They seemed to be working in tandem: one was watching Ron and the other was scanning the room.

"Look at those two guys," Lucy whispered to Sue. "Who do you think they are?"

Sue shrugged. "Tourists?"

"Look again. They're definitely interested in Ron."

They watched as Andy Dorfman entered the coffee shop and headed for Ron's table, where he sat down. The two men at the next table suddenly appeared to be very interested in their menus. Lucy jumped to a conclusion. "I bet they're bodyguards."

Sue stared at her. "Now it's my turn to get worried," she said. "First you decide I'm in danger from my husband of almost thirty years, and now you think two perfectly ordinary young men are bodyguards or something. You've got some imagination there."

"I wish it was my imagination," said Lucy. "I wouldn't be at all surprised if he'd hired some protection. Things are really tense down at the harbor. There was almost a big fight yesterday. Ron doesn't want the fishermen using the dock, because the noise and the smell upset Thelma."

"I'd like to upset Thelma. Come on, Lucy, you must have some ideas. How can I get this wedding back on track?"

Lucy watched as Dorfman set a tiny tape recorder on the table and began talking with Ron, apparently interviewing him. Down at the harbor, thought Lucy, it had been easy to underestimate Davitz. He had seemed like the unpopular kid in the schoolyard, being picked on by the bigger, more athletic kids. It was easy to forget how wealthy and powerful, and well-connected, he really was.

"She ought to be pleased with her little boy today—it looks like he's doing that magazine interview she wanted." Lucy smiled.

Sue smiled back. It was the first time since they'd started talking, Lucy realized.

"You know, on one hand I think it's great that Sidra's going to be meeting all these important people and having so many opportunities. Then on the other hand, I can't help wondering if she really knows what she's getting into."

"Which brings us back to Ron," said Lucy, watching as he suddenly stood up, knocking over his chair.

The commotion attracted everyone's attention; there was a sudden silence, and all eyes were on him as he marched out the door.

"I guess Dorfman got a little too personal," said Lucy. She picked up her previous train of thought. "Sue, you're forgetting that Sidra has been living in New York for a couple of years now and working on the TV show. She's already living in a much different world from Tinker's Cove."

Out of the corner of her eye, Lucy saw movement and turned to focus on it. One of the muscular young men was on his feet. "Look! One of those guys is following Ron!" She savored the moment. "So, who's got an overactive imagination now?"

"He's probably going next door to buy postcards," said Sue.

"And his friend is going to help him carry them," retorted Lucy as the second man stood up and took the check over to the cash register.

"Whatever," sighed Sue wearily. "Maybe I should just give up and let Thelma do whatever she wants. It looks like she's going to do it anyway."

"Things have a way of working out." Lucy knew she was simply repeating a platitude, when something occurred to her. "Sidra will be coming home for the shower, won't she?"

"Of course."

"Well, this is your opportunity to find out what she wants. She's your ace in the hole, you know. If she is appalled and horrified by the shower . . ."

"She will be." Sue was certain.

"Then you can team up against Thelma. . . ."

"And get back the wedding!"

Sue jumped out of her chair. "Lucy, you're a genius!"

"About time people realized it," muttered Lucy, reaching for the check. She glanced at it and handed it to Sue. "This one's on you."

Chapter Ten

The invitation to the shower didn't arrive until Saturday. As usual, Lucy was cleaning, and today she had the house almost to herself because Bill and Elizabeth were working and Sara and Zoe were visiting friends. Only Toby was home, sound asleep. A typical college kid, he slept until noon whenever he got the chance.

She had just finished wiping down the kitchen counters when she looked out and saw that the little red flag on the mailbox was down. She trotted down the driveway to get the mail, and there among the bills and credit card offers was a little square envelope.

She opened it as she walked up the drive to the house, and a handful of variously colored cards tumbled out and fell to the ground. Lucy stooped to pick them up and discovered they were cards from the stores where Sidra and Ron had registered their wedding gift preferences. They were all in New York, and the only one Lucy recognized was Tiffany's.

As she stood there flipping through the cards, she felt a curious mix of emotions. Did they really want her company at the shower, or were they just after a gift? A rather expensive gift at that, judging from the cards.

And why did they think they had to tell her where to shop? It was insulting, and furthermore, it made her feel inadequate. Even if she wanted to—and she realized guiltily that she didn't want to—how could she afford a gift from Tiffany's?

Replacing the cards in the envelope, she studied the invitation. The shower was to be on the yacht, on the evening of July 4. A handwritten PS invited her to stay for the fireworks in the harbor.

Now that was better, thought Lucy. It would be fun to see the fireworks from the boat. And no doubt there would be plenty of delicious food, and it would be lovely to see Sidra again and meet her friends from New York.

In the kitchen, Lucy attached the invitation to the refrigerator with a magnet. Then she reached under the sink for her bucket of cleaning supplies. She still had to clean the bathrooms and dust and vacuum the downstairs. The upstairs would have to wait until after lunch.

She was making herself a sandwich in her sparkling kitchen when Toby appeared, looking disheveled and seeking coffee.

"It will have to be instant," she told him.

"Fine with me," he said, slumping into a chair at the kitchen table and reaching for the morning paper.

She finished making her sandwich and fixed him a cup of coffee. When she leaned over him to place it in front of him at the table, she got a whiff of alcohol.

"Big night last night?" she demanded, hands on her hips.

"What do you mean?"

"I can tell you were drinking. Which, by the way, is not a good idea since you're underage and you shouldn't drive. . . ."

"Mom, how could I drive? I don't have a car. Friends brought me home."

"Who? Eddie? He's underage, too."

"Some of the guys from the Bilge."

Lucy's eyebrows shot up. The Bilge was the most disreputable bar in town, located just a few feet from the harbor. It was also, she remembered, the place where the fishermen had agreed to meet to plan their protest against the new harbor policy.

"So what were you doing at the Bilge?"

"I went with Geoff, for a meeting."

"Geoff bought you beer?" Lucy was astonished.

"No. I bought myself beer."

"Considering the way you smell, you bought a lot of beer."

Toby shrugged. "He left early. I stayed." He swallowed some coffee. "Do we have any aspirin?"

Lucy fought the urge to get up and bring him aspirin. "There's some in the medicine cabinet in the bathroom."

Toby absorbed this information but didn't act on it. Tough, thought Lucy. He deserves a hangover.

"Anything interesting happen at the meeting?" she asked, keeping her tone carefully casual.

"Nah."

This was like pulling teeth, thought Lucy. "Were they putting something together for the waterways commission meeting on Monday?"

Toby was peering in the refrigerator, probably hoping for a slice of cold pizza or some leftover spaghetti. He settled for some orange juice and pulled the container out. "Not exactly," he said, tilting the container and pouring the juice into his mouth. Lucy would have made a fuss, but she knew the container was nearly empty.

"But I thought they're unhappy with the new transient policy."

"Oh, they are. But they figure going to the meeting will be pointless. They've got something else in mind."

He tossed the empty container in the garbage and headed for the bathroom.

"Like what?"

"Sorry. I promised."

Lucy found herself talking to a closed door. "Promised what?"

The door opened a crack. "Promised not to tell you." Then it closed again and she heard the shower.

Irritated, she put her plate and glass in the dishwasher and slammed it shut. It didn't seem fair. She fed and clothed and educated him—at great expense. The least he could do was pass along a hot news tip.

Later that afternoon, Lucy was reclining on the chaise longue in the gazebo. Her conscience was clear. After cleaning the entire house, she deserved a rest. Kudo seemed to agree; he was stretched across the top step, making sure no one would disturb her.

When Bill's pickup turned in the drive, he leapt to his feet and went to meet him with his tail wagging. A few minutes later, they both joined her. Bill had changed out of his work clothes and was carrying a beer.

"This is peaceful," he said, sitting down.

"I'm pooped," said Lucy. "I cleaned the whole house."

"You wouldn't have to do it all in one day if you weren't working full-time," he said.

Lucy shrugged. She didn't want to argue.

"How's the boathouse going?" she asked.

Bill was currently restoring a nineteenth-century boathouse for some summer people who owned one of the big "cottages" overlooking the water on Smith Heights Road.

"Good," he said, gazing out across the yard to the mountains. "You know, I heard the oddest thing today. From the porta-potty guy."

Lucy dropped her magazine.

"He said you'd ordered a couple of porta-potties for the first weekend in August," continued Bill. "Lucy, why did you do that?"

"For the wedding." Lucy's voice was very small.

"What wedding?"

"Sue wants to have Sidra's wedding here. Right here in the gazebo. Won't that be nice?"

Bill narrowed his eyes. "And when were you going to tell me?"

"I am telling you. Now you know."

Bill took a long drink. "I live here, too, you know. It would be nice if you'd checked with me first, don't you think?"

"I figured you'd be excited about it. It's a *wedding*. Everyone loves weddings. It's a big honor."

Bill sighed. "How much is this honor going to cost me?"

Lucy smiled at him. "Either a lot or nothing. Thelma—she's the mother of the groom—wants to have it at the Hadwen House."

"Go, Thelma," said Bill.

Lucy laughed.

On Monday morning Lucy was already at her desk, working on the lobster story, when Phyllis arrived.

"Did you get an invitation?" asked Phyllis as she stashed her purse in the bottom drawer of her desk.

"Sure did."

"Well, I hope they don't think I'm going to buy a shower gift from Tiffany's!"

"You're not?" Lucy feigned surprise.

Phyllis stared at her. "No, I'm not. I'm heading straight for K-Mart after work. I'm going to get some of those cute Martha Stewart dish towels. They look vintage, but they're new."

"Those are nice," agreed Lucy. "I don't have any ideas.

Especially since I'll be getting her a wedding present, too." She sighed. "I want to get her something nice; I really do."

"No problem. Just call Tiffany's. They even gave you the phone number."

"It was thoughtful of them," said Lucy sarcastically. "But these days, even K-Mart is a stretch for me. Tuition's due in August, you know."

"You're always picking up stuff at yard sales. Why don't you give her something from your collection?"

Lucy was intrigued.

"Can I do that?"

Phyllis shrugged. "Why not?"

"I did find a set of those nesting Pyrex bowls at a yard sale last month. . . ."

"The red and yellow and blue ones? Those are hot now."

"I got the whole set for five dollars."

"That was a steal."

"I know." Lucy smiled smugly, thinking of how she had arranged the bowls on the top shelf of the pantry where they were part of a growing collection of 1950s kitchenware. She really loved those bowls.

"Why not give her those?"

"I couldn't," said Lucy, resisting the idea. They were her bowls and she didn't want to part with them.

"Not in good shape?"

"Mint," Lucy admitted. "I don't think they were ever used."

"I don't see the problem," said Phyllis, reaching for the phone.

Lucy sat silently, wrestling with her conscience. The voice of her Sunday school teacher, Mrs. Pilling, whispered in her ear. "It is better to give than to receive." She groaned out loud.

Phyllis had finished talking on the phone. "Are you all right?" she asked.

"Okay, okay. Sidra gets the bowls."

Phyllis beamed at her. "That's a really nice gift, and they'll go great with my dishtowels."

The door opened, making the little bell jingle, and Ted walked in.

Lucy and Phyllis immediately busied themselves at their desks.

"Now, this is more like it," he said, setting his briefcase on a chair. "Monday morning, everybody's at work, nobody's talking about weddings."

Lucy pursed her lips together tightly, but a little giggle escaped from Phyllis.

That night Lucy went to the waterways commission, confident that she wouldn't mix up any names. Ted had coached her before letting her leave the office.

"The chairman is Wilfred Wiggins."

"Frank's uncle."

"Right. The members are Henry Wiggins—"

"Frank's cousin?"

"Yes. Then there's Alf Cobb—he's married to Wilfred's daughter Clara."

"Cousin-in-law."

Ted wasn't sure. "Whatever. Alf's missing a couple of fingers. Winch accident."

"Got it."

"Then there's two older men, retirees. Al Sklar, who used to run the boatyard, and Herb Mason. You can't miss him. Even when he's on land he looks like he ought to be on a boat."

"I've got a feeling this is going to be interesting. Toby told me the fishermen are planning some kind of protest."

"Just remember to keep your head down. Those guys can get rough."

"Okay."

But when Lucy arrived at the meeting room in the basement of town hall, nobody was there but the commissioners and a few regulars, mostly retirees who made a hobby of attending meetings.

As she waited for the meeting to begin, she studied the commissioners. Wilfred Wiggins, the chairman, bore a strong resemblance to Frank. His hair was the same reddish color, only there was less of it, and he didn't have a mustache. He had the same wiry body, however, and a prominent Adam's apple.

Tom Wiggins wasn't Wilfred's son, Lucy knew; he was his nephew. Tom's mother was Alf's sister, and she had apparently married someone with black hair. Tom had a full head of thick, dark hair and a stocky build.

Alf Cobb was only related to the Wigginses by marriage, but oddly enough, with his sandy hair and bad teeth he could have been mistaken for Frank's brother.

The three men obviously enjoyed each other's company. They were chuckling over something, and their attitude made Lucy feel a bit like an intruder. The other two board members seemed to feel the same way, for they were seated together at the end of the table, occasionally commenting to each other.

At seven o'clock, Wilfred Wiggins pounded his gavel on the table and called the meeting to order, even though the harbormaster had not yet arrived. The committee had waived the reading of the minutes of the last meeting and approved them and dealt with some old business when Frank appeared, dressed in a freshly pressed uniform.

"I'm sorry I'm late," he said, blinking his eyes and twitching his shoulders.

Wilfred didn't ask for an explanation but smiled indulgently. "Got held up, did ya? Well, it goes with the job. Always something."

Lucy suspected Frank had gotten held up at the laundromat, but the board members did not appear to share her suspicions.

"Not a problem, not a problem," said Tom, baring his brown and ragged teeth in a smile.

"Let's hear your report; then we'll see if the board members have any questions. Agreed?"

All the board members nodded their heads.

Frank pulled a piece of paper out of his pocket and took his place in front of the table, where he stood, jiggling on his toes. He began reading.

"Harbormaster's report for the month of June. Commercial boats: sixteen. Recreational boats: forty-eight. Prorated income from resident users: ten thousand one hundred and sixty-six dollars. Income from transients: twelve thousand dollars."

He stood for a moment, Adam's apple bobbing furiously, waiting for the board's reaction.

"I guess that twelve thousand is from that big yacht," said Wilfred.

"That's a nice boat," said Herb.

"I'll bet that baby takes plenty of fuel," said Al with a little whistle.

"He can afford it," observed Tom. "They say he's the next Bill Gates."

"Must be somethin' to have a boat like that," said Herb, fingering his Quisset Point Yacht Club hat. Despite its name, Lucy knew the boats at the yacht club were hardly yachts; they were mostly day-sailers and a few small power boats.

"Do I have a motion to accept the harbormaster's report?" asked Wilfred.

"I so move," said Tom.

"I second it," said Alf.

"Vote?" asked Wilfred.

"Hold yer horses," said Herb, and Lucy pricked up her ears. "You forgot discussion."

"Any discussion?"

Herb looked pointedly at Al, and Lucy wondered if dissension would actually erupt at the meeting.

"Well, uh," began Al, looking uncomfortable, "last month we voted on a new policy to, uh, encourage transient use, and I wondered how it was going. Any problems?"

"Good point," acceded Wilfred. "Any problems, Frank?"

Lucy sat at attention, waiting to hear Wiggins's answer. Would he acknowledge that the fishermen were angry about the new policy, or would he cover it up?

Frank stood for a few minutes, staring at the ceiling. Then he looked down at his shoes. A shudder ran through his body and he swallowed. "Nope," he said.

Interesting, thought Lucy. She suspected word of last week's confrontation had reached some of the board members. Would they challenge Wiggins, or would they accept his word?

"That's fine, then," said Wilfred. "I have a motion to accept the harbormaster's report. All in favor?"

Everyone was in favor.

"We have one other order of business," began Wilfred. "As you all know, Friday is the Fourth of July and we always have a fireworks display in the harbor. Is everything set for that?"

"All set," replied Frank, nodding his head and blinking rapidly.

"Do I have a motion to adjourn?"

Lucy checked her watch. At barely fifteen minutes, it was the briefest meeting she'd ever covered. Maybe nepotism wasn't all bad, she thought as she stuffed her notebook in her purse and made her way through the rows of folding chairs.

More chairs than usual, she thought, surveying the room. Maybe the janitor had outdone himself, or maybe the commission had been expecting a larger turnout. At the door, she paused. She knew the fishermen had been planning something at the Bilge, but not a single one had shown up at the meeting. What were they going to do?

Chapter Eleven

Independence Day was always celebrated in grand style in Tinker's Cove, and the parade was as big a highlight of the day as the fireworks display in the harbor. Preparations were well underway; Lucy noticed that flags and bunting had appeared on many of the Main Street stores when she went to work on Tuesday. The town certainly had a festive air, but Lucy didn't think that could account for Ted's cheerful attitude. He was whistling a happy little tune, sitting in his usual spot at the enormous rolltop desk he'd inherited from his grandfather.

"You seem awfully chipper today," she commented as she waited for her computer to boot up. The groans and clicks emanating from the aged machine seemed to indicate she was asking it to do an awful lot.

"Biggest issue ever—forty-eight pages," he replied.

Lucy knew it was advertising, not news, that determined the size of the paper.

"Business must be good."

"You betcha. And it looks like next week will be just as good. How did the meeting go?"

"Fast. It went very fast. It was over before it began."

"The fishermen didn't show up?"

"No," said Lucy slowly. "But I've heard rumors they've got some sort of protest planned."

Ted snorted. "That'll be the day. Those guys couldn't organize a protest if they tried. They're all captains, if you know what I mean. When everybody's giving the orders and nobody's taking them, it's hard to get much done."

Lucy laughed. "Not to mention the fact that they all spend way too much time in the Bilge." She paused. "Now Toby's discovered the place."

Ted shook his head sympathetically. "You better warn him. He'll get in trouble if he hangs around there."

They both knew that the Bilge appeared frequently in the police log they printed every week.

"I told him, but I don't think he listened."

"They gotta learn the hard way."

Lucy nodded and glanced at the clock. It was after nine and there was no sign of Phyllis.

"Is Phyllis off today?"

"No."

"Then she's late."

"Impossible."

"Maybe she's sick."

"She hasn't called, and she was fine yesterday."

"Maybe she had car trouble," speculated Lucy, opening her notebook and starting her report on the meeting. She was almost done when the door flew open and Phyllis marched in, nearly an hour late, looking rather flustered.

"What happened?"

Phyllis didn't pause for breath. "I was just driving along minding my own business when I saw my cousin Elfrida coming the other way. She was on South Street and there wasn't any traffic to speak of, so we stopped to chat a minute."

Lucy knew that folks in Tinker's Cove thought nothing of pulling their cars alongside for a conversation. If she herself came upon two motorists so engaged and blocking traffic, she didn't mind—as long as the chat didn't last too long.

"Well," Phyllis continued, "Elfrida was just starting to tell me about Aunt Effie's new boyfriend when—bam!—somebody drove smack into my car. Rear-ended me! Can you believe it?"

"Are you hurt?"

"I'm all right—my back is stiffening up a bit, but I'm okay."

"What about the car?"

"My Buick? Just fine, thank you. But you should see the other car, the car that hit me. It's one of those rice burners. The fender was hanging off and the bumper was all screwed up." Phyllis's tone was triumphant. "I guess he got what he deserved, driving like that."

"Who was it?"

"That magazine writer. The one who was in here last week. Doing the story on the next Bill Gates."

"Dorfman?"

"That's it. And wasn't he fit to be tied! Acting like it was my fault or something. Said he never heard of people just stopping in the middle of the road. Imagine!"

"He does come from New York." Lucy didn't think New York drivers would tolerate traffic delays while motorists stopped to gossip. "So, who's Aunt Effie's new boyfriend?"

"I never did find out!"

Lucy chuckled and went back to work on her story, quickly finishing it up. Since she had plenty of time, she was also able to work on her lobster story.

"You know, if you've got a lot of room in the paper, I think I can have the story on the lobster project ready by tomorrow," she told Ted.

Ted was cautious. "I don't want to rush you."

"Really, it's almost ready."

"Well, I could use it."

"It's all yours."

* * *

"That story you wrote about Geoff Rumford's research project was nice work."

Lucy, who was sitting on one of the rocking chairs on the front porch at the Queen Vic Inn, looked up and saw Andy Dorfman. It was the Fourth of July. She'd brought a resentful Elizabeth to work and was sitting for a few minutes, watching the crowds of people gathering for the parade.

"Thanks." Lucy was genuinely pleased at this praise. After all, Dorfman worked for a national publication. "How's your car?"

"You heard about that? News really travels fast in this town."

"Phyllis, the woman you hit, works at the paper."

"Oh." He stood for a moment with his hands shoved in his shorts pockets. "Beats me how people can just stop in the middle of the street."

"Local custom," said Lucy. "How's your story going? The one about the next Bill Gates."

"The subject's not cooperating," said Dorfman.

"I saw him throw a fit in the doughnut shop." Lucy paused. She was dying to get the inside scoop on Davitz, but she knew she couldn't be too direct without trespassing on Dorfman's research. "I bet his mother wasn't pleased," she ventured with a little chuckle.

"Turns out he's not quite the mama's boy he appears to be." Dorfman grinned wickedly. "The mouth on that boy! I was shocked."

Lucy laughed, hoping to encourage him to elaborate. "Personally, I'm glad to hear it. It's my opinion that that woman has too much influence over her son."

"Never fear," said Dorfman, declining to respond and adroitly changing the subject. "Are you staying to watch the parade?"

Lucy leaned back and rocked in the comfortable chair. "I wish. Unfortunately, Mrs. McNaughton has already given me the evil eye once or twice. I'm related to the help, you see. My daughter works here."

"Not that cute little chambermaid with the bad attitude?"

"You got it. Getting her here this morning was quite a struggle. I'm just resting here for a few minutes, trying to summon the energy to find the rest of the family." She narrowed her eyes mischievously. "Tell you what. I'll give you a real good deal on this chair. Just tell me how Davitz got a great girl like Sidra to fall in love with him."

"That's simple," he said. "Money talks."

"She's not that kind of girl," protested Lucy.

"Trust me, they're all that kind of girl."

"Not Sidra," insisted Lucy.

She stood up and offered him the chair with a flourish, then hopped down the porch steps and sauntered down the street, keeping an eye out for Bill and the girls. As she walked she also looked for Toby, who'd said he would be watching with his friends, but she didn't see any sign of him. The parade was supposed to begin in just a few minutes, and the sidewalk was full of observers, most of them dressed in variations of red, white, and blue. Many were holding small flags or sporting straw hats with patriotic ribbons. Small children had little flags painted on their cheeks.

When she found her family, Lucy was dismayed to see they'd staked out viewing territory right in front of the *Pennysaver* office.

"I can't ever get away from this place," she moaned, but her complaints were cut off by the siren of a police car announcing the beginning of the parade.

Riding behind the cruiser, in an open convertible, was the grand marshal, Franny Small. Franny was an old friend of Lucy's who had managed the hardware store for years, until it was driven out of business by competition from a national chain. Franny had started making jewelry out of the remaining stock of nuts and bolts and had been hugely successful. She was now one of the town's top employers.

"Hi, Franny!" screamed Lucy, waving her arm.

Franny turned and, spotting Sara and Zoe, tossed a handful of hard candy their way, setting off a scramble among the children in the vicinity.

The grand marshal's car was followed by a group of girl scouts holding signs announcing the theme of the parade: liberty and justice for all.

"Pretty controversial," joked Bill, standing at attention as the boy scouts' color guard passed by, followed by a girl dressed as the Statue of Liberty.

Even though she had covered her body with green paint, her toga was revealing, and Lucy wondered if his attention was entirely patriotic.

Several Scottish pipers were next, prompting Sara and Zoe to join in an impromptu jig. Their dance was rewarded with more candy, tossed their way by a clown on a unicycle. A float created by the local nursery came next: a garden had been created on a flatbed trailer, and several employees were lounging in hammocks and lawn furniture. "LIBERTY AND JUSTICE—AND SUNSHINE—FOR ALL," read a placard on the side of the float.

It was definitely popular with the crowd. Everyone clapped as it passed, and Lucy thought it had a real chance of winning the chamber of commerce's trophy for most creative entry.

A group of aged veterans, in bits and pieces of uniform, followed the float. They were no longer the trim, young fellows who had marched off to fight in World War II, but they were still standing tall despite potbellies and stiff joints.

Again Lucy and Bill were on their feet, showing respect to these veterans who had saved the world from fascism.

The veterans were followed by a pickup towing a dory on a trailer. The antique wooden dory, beautifully refinished, was filled with kids enrolled in the sailing program at Point Quisset Yacht Club. Mostly the children of wealthy summer folk, the kids were all dressed in matching PQYC polo shirts and blue shorts. With their sun-streaked hair and tans and white teeth, Lucy suspected the sun shone a little brighter on them than on some local children.

This suspicion was confirmed with the appearance of the high school marching band. It was a poor showing since many of the kids couldn't get away from their summer jobs, and the few who had shown up were dressed in worn and faded polyester uniforms. Sweat was pouring down their faces. But even though the band was off-tempo and out of tune, they got an enthusiastic welcome from the crowd.

That welcome turned to silence, and then bursts of raucous laughter, as the next float appeared. Perched on a flatbed trailer towed by a shiny truck tractor was a huge, gleaming white model of Ron Davitz's yacht. Two men were on the yacht: a yachtsman dressed in a cap and a blue blazer with money bulging from every pocket, and a caricature of Frank Wiggins dressed in a harbormaster's uniform and a red clown's wig. The harbormaster figure was on all fours, carrying the yachtsman on his back. Standing by and applauding were five more figures, supposedly the members of the waterways commission. A sign along the side of the trailer read: "LIBERTY AND JUSTICE FOR ALL—IF THEY CAN PAY."

Bill nudged Lucy. "Is that Toby?"

Lucy took a closer look, and sure enough, it was Toby under the costume and makeup of the yachtsman.

"So that's what he's been up to all those nights at the Bilge."

"If you ask me, it's pretty funny," said Bill.

The float was getting a mixed reaction from the crowd. Vacationers and visitors didn't quite know what to make of it, but the locals roared their approval. The children in the crowd were having a great time, trying to catch the play money Toby was tossing their way.

Across the street, Lucy caught a glimpse of Frank Wiggins, looking absolutely furious.

"It may be funny," agreed Lucy, "but I don't think it's going to win any prizes."

"Too bad," said Bill, handing her one of the bogus bills.

Lucy fingered it thoughtfully. Considering what she knew of Frank Wiggins and Ron Davitz, neither was the type to take such public mockery with a grain of salt. Somebody would pay for this. She hoped it wasn't going to be Toby.

Chapter Twelve

Lucy felt a little odd as she drove off to the shower later that day in the Subaru, the wrapped Pyrex bowls set carefully on the passenger seat. The Fourth of July had always been a family holiday with a cookout followed by the fireworks, but this year Elizabeth and Toby had made plans with their friends, and Lucy had been invited to the shower.

Left with only the two younger girls, Bill had accepted an invitation to the Orensteins' barbecue. Lucy knew they'd have a good time, but she still felt a little guilty about going to the shower all by herself.

On the other hand, she admitted to herself, wild horses couldn't have kept her away. Sue needed her moral support—that went without saying—but this was also an opportunity to see Thelma in action. Lucy couldn't begin to imagine what she had planned for the shower. Anything could happen. Entertainment by Chippendale's? Siegfried and Roy and assorted feline companions? The Rolling Stones dropping by to play an unplugged private concert? Nothing seemed too outrageous for Thelma, given her access to her son's money and her willingness to spend it.

As she drove, she cast a nervous eye on the sky, where

clouds were gathering. The spell of fine weather they'd been enjoying was finally coming to an end; thunderstorms had been forecast, and she hoped they'd hold off until after the fireworks.

When Lucy pulled into the parking lot at the harbor, the Davitzes' yacht was brightly lit with Christmas lights—even the gangplank was outlined in twinkling white lights. As she drew closer, she could hear the buzz of conversation and the tinkle of piano music. For a moment, she felt like pinching herself. The warm night air, the music, the graceful figures on the deck—she felt as if she had wandered into *The Great Gatsby.*

Stepping on board the Sea Witch, she was met by a uniformed steward, who welcomed her and relieved her of her gift, placing it with others on a nearby table. She then made her way to the open deck on the stern, where the guests were gathered, and looked for her hostess.

She didn't find Thelma, but she did see Sue and Sidra and hurried right over, embracing Sidra and giving her a big hug.

"It's wonderful to see you—and such a happy occasion. You know we all wish you so much happiness."

"It's nice to see you, too, Aunt Lucy," replied Sidra.

Lucy studied her, realizing again just how much she resembled her mother. She had Sue's neat, petite body and her straight, glossy hair. Her face was softer and plumper than her mother's; where Sue's lean features made her striking, Sidra was pretty—even beautiful.

"You look wonderful, a beautiful bride," said Lucy. "I can't get over how much you look like your mother."

"That's the last thing she wants to hear," said Sue, an edge to her voice.

"Nonsense. I could've done a lot worse." Sidra sounded as if she were going through the motions, repeating platitudes, thought Lucy, watching as she turned to greet another guest.

"C'mon, I'll show you where the bar is," offered Sue.

"Where's Thelma? I haven't had a chance to say hi."

"She was here a minute ago." Sue shrugged. "Must have flown off on her broomstick."

Lucy didn't like the sound of this. She wondered if the mother-and-daughter reunion hadn't gone quite the way Sue wanted.

"You seem a little upset," she said. "What's going on?"

"I'll have a gin and tonic, light on the tonic," said Sue, stepping up to the bar. "Lucy, what'll you have?"

"White wine."

As soon as the drinks were set before them, Sue tossed hers back in one long swallow and replaced the glass. "I'll have another."

Lucy took her hand and realized she was trembling. "Hold on a minute—tell me what's wrong."

"I'm a wreck. My God, I need another drink."

Lucy glanced at the bartender, who had raised a questioning eyebrow.

"Okay," she said, nodding. "But then you have to tell me what's wrong."

Lucy picked up the fresh drink before Sue could grab it and led her to a quiet corner next to the bar. "Talk," she said, handing her the drink.

Sue took a quavery breath. "The gun—you know, the one I hid—is gone."

This was the last thing Lucy expected to hear.

"Do you think Sid found it?"

"Who else?"

"Did you ask him about it?"

Sue looked at her as if she were crazy. "I didn't tell him I hid it, so how could I tell him it was gone."

"I think you need to talk to him about this."

"No." Sue was adamant. Her glass, Lucy noticed, was again empty.

"Now, what are you two doing conspiring in the corners?" demanded Thelma, descending on them in a dress comprised of layers and layers of fluttery chiffon accessorized with ropes and ropes of twinkling stones.

Diamonds? wondered Lucy, embarrassed to be found behaving so unsociably by her hostess.

"Such a lovely party—" she began, only to be interrupted by Sue.

"We were just getting drinks," she said, turning her back on Thelma and marching to the bar.

Lucy tried to cover her friend's rudeness. "Is Ron going to be here tonight?"

It was the wrong thing to say.

"He was supposed to be, but he hasn't shown up yet." Thelma was clearly annoyed, but she gave a little chuckle. "Isn't that just like a man?"

Unbidden, an image of Ron appeared to Lucy. He was clutching his chest, which was bleeding, and Sid was standing over him, holding a smoking gun. Lucy blinked, and found herself staring at Thelma's raccoon eyes.

"Just like a man," repeated Lucy.

"Well, I hope he gets here in time to open the presents," said Thelma, bustling off to welcome a new arrival.

Lucy turned her attention to Sue, who was feeling the effects of her drinks.

"Come on, let's join the party," she said, taking Sue by the elbow.

"Let'sh no'," said Sue, leaning heavily on her arm.

As Lucy led her back to the deck, Lucy wondered how many drinks she'd had. This wasn't like Sue, who rarely drank more than a glass of white wine at a time. Lucy looked for a chair, noticing that the party had divided into two camps: a cluster of women in pastel dresses represented the home team, while a group dressed almost identically in black sleeveless shifts seemed to be the New Yorkers. Lucy decided to cross the great divide and led Sue to a seat by the New York crowd.

"You must be one of the bridesmaids," she said, extending a hand to a very thin girl with very long hair. "I'm Lucy Stone, an old friend of the family."

"How nice," said the girl, turning around and tossing her hair in Lucy's face.

"That's Susanna. She works with Sidra," said Sue. "C'mon. Let's go talk to Rachel and Pam."

Seeing that the New Yorkers had closed ranks around Sidra, Lucy followed Sue's unsteady progress to the other side of the boat. There, Rachel Goodman and Ted's wife Pam were chatting with Phyllis.

"You can say what you want about Thelma," said Rachel in a low voice, "but the woman sure knows how to throw a party."

"Look at these shrimp." Phyllis held up a skewer. "They're huge."

"And these little crab cakes—delish!" added Pam.

"Good idea," said Lucy, thinking that Sue could use some solid food.

"Not hungry," said Sue. "Thirshy."

Lucy shook her head, and Pam, taking in the situation, grabbed Sue's other arm.

"C'mon, Sue. Let's take a turn round the buffet table."

Between the two of them they got Sue to the table, but when Lucy let go of her arm to reach for a plate, she wriggled away and disappeared into the crowd.

"We tried," said Pam. "How much has she had?"

"Too much," said Lucy. "Should I have the bartender cut her off?"

"Not the way she is now. She'd just raise a ruckus. With luck she'll find a quiet spot and pass out."

"And if not," said Lucy, "she'll raise holy hell." She studied the lavish buffet and came to a decision. "Whatever happens, I'll probably need nourishment."

"That's the spirit," said Pam. "Oooh, these stuffed mushrooms are fabulous."

"Mmm," agreed Lucy.

"It's time for the gifts," announced Thelma, trotting around on her high heels and waving her arms as if she were performing an odd little dance of the seven veils in her layered dress. "Everyone take a seat."

It took a few minutes for the group to get settled, forming a sort of circle around Sidra. There was still no sign of Ron, and Lucy didn't blame him. He would have been the only man present and would certainly have felt rather awkward. Thelma clapped and a steward appeared, carrying a tray of gifts. He was followed by another, and another, until the pile of wrapped presents set before Sidra towered above her.

"Oh, my goodness," exclaimed the bride-to-be, as a little color rose in her cheeks. "This is too much. It's embarrassing."

"At least she has the decency to blush," observed Phyllis, a touch of vinegar in her voice. "Where's Sue?"

"Sleeping it off, I hope," said Lucy. She was worried about Sue, but didn't feel she could absent herself from the group without being conspicuous.

"Now, who's this from?" Sidra had plucked a large box from the pile and was opening the card. "From Susanna. I know this is going to be lovely."

"Who is Susanna?" hissed Pam.

"One of the WIBs," replied Rachel. "Women in black."

Sidra was pulling the gift from waves of tissue paper, revealing a Cuisinart. Everybody oohed.

"Oh, you shouldn't have. Thank you so much. . . ."

Sidra was interrupted by Molly Thacher, her old high school friend. "Now, Sidra, what did you do with the bow?"

Sidra fumbled with the discarded wrapping and found the bow.

"What do you want with it?"

"Why, she's going to make a hat, just like they did at my baby shower," said Carrie Swift, Chuck's wife. "They made me the cutest hat by taping all the bows to a paper plate."

"Oh," said Sidra, with a conspicuous lack of enthusiasm.

"I'll make the hat if you just give me a paper plate," offered Molly.

"Too bad. No paper plates," said one of the WIBs, throwing her hands in the air.

Molly and Carrie shared a glance.

"Next present," announced the third WIB, passing a huge box to Sidra.

There were more oohs and aahs when this gift—a crystal punch bowl—was revealed.

"Oh, Lily! It isn't Waterford, is it?"

Lily smiled demurely and nodded.

"You darling! You shouldn't have!"

"Darn tootin' she shouldn't have," muttered Phyllis. "What's Sidra going to do with a white elephant like that?"

Lucy shrugged and bit her tongue. She wasn't going to tell Phyllis how much that particular white elephant had cost.

"Now, what could this be?"

Sidra was holding up a flat little package, simply wrapped in tissue paper and white, curling ribbon.

"Oh, that's mine!" exclaimed Molly.

All eyes were on Sidra as she unwrapped the gift: four handwoven potholders in violent shades of purple and pink.

"What are . . ." began one WIB.

"Like you make in camp," volunteered the second WIB.

"On a little loom!" finished the third, dissolving into helpless giggles.

"I made them myself," Molly volunteered, puzzled at the reaction to her gift. "I used your favorite colors. Remember, in eighth grade, you said you were going to have an all-pink house?"

"Really, you shouldn't have," exclaimed Sidra. From her tone, it seemed clear she wasn't pleased to be reminded of her childhood excesses.

"No expense spared!" hooted the first WIB.

"One hundred percent synthetic!" added another.

"Your favorite colors!" shrilled the third.

"Well, I think they're very pretty," Carrie said, patting Molly's hand.

Molly's head was bowed and Lucy hoped she wasn't crying. They're not worth your tears, she wanted to tell her.

"Ah, a present from Kat . . . I bet it's going to be naughty," said Sidra as she untied the bow and lifted the top off the next box. When she saw what was inside, she shrieked.

"What could it be?" Pam wondered aloud.

"A sexy nightie?" Lucy guessed.

"Not quite," Rachel said drily as Sidra held up a black leather mask, a whip, and a pair of gloves.

"It's the whole outfit," volunteered Kat. "Just in case Ron gets out of hand."

The women on the boat were silent. Even Thelma seemed at a loss for words, choosing instead to fan herself with a napkin.

"What size do these come in, anyway?" asked one of the WIBs.

"Mean, meaner and meanest," replied Kat, sending Sidra and the other WIBs into gales of laughter.

Lucy decided to take advantage of the moment to slip away and look for Sue. She found her, predictably, at the bar. Perched on a stool, she was telling the bartender all about her troubles.

"Jusht don' reck, reckanize my own daughter," said Sue, shaking her head sadly. "The lil girl I raised wouldn't ack like thish."

"How's it going?" asked Lucy, taking the seat beside her.

"Know tha' movie—*Vasion of the Body Sna-snashhers?* Thass wha's happened. They've snashed Sidra. She looksh like Sidra and talksh like Sidra, but she's not."

From what Lucy had seen, she thought Sue might be on to something. "Did you talk to her about the wedding plans?"

Sue nodded and drained the last of her drink.

"She sez whatever Thelma wansh is fine with her—doesn't want to alee—aleenate her mother"—Sue hiccuped—"in-law." She passed her drink to the bartender. "Fill 'er up."

In response to his glance, Lucy mouthed the word "tonic." He nodded in understanding and made the drink without adding any gin.

Sue took a swallow and Lucy held her breath.

"Mmm, good," said Sue.

"C'mon," said Lucy, standing up. "Let's go up to the top deck and get a good spot for the fireworks. They'll be starting soon."

"Goo' idea."

Sue wasn't too steady on her feet, but Lucy managed to get her up the stairs and out into the fresh air. From below, they could hear the women's voices as Sidra worked her way through the pile of presents, but they had the upper deck to themselves. Lucy led Sue to a pair of deck chairs by the railing and they sat down, looking out over the harbor. A crowd had gathered in the parking lot and on the hills around the harbor, but Lucy and Sue couldn't see them from where they sat. A few boats bobbed about, filled with people waiting for the fireworks to start, but for the most part the harbor was dark and peaceful. The water gleamed black with silver reflections from the lights on the boats. Anytime now the fireworks would start.

Lucy noticed Sue's head drooping. At last, she was finally drifting off. Sitting beside her, Lucy took a moment to reflect. She could imagine how she would feel if Elizabeth behaved as Sidra had, and how horrified she would be if her college friends turned out to be like the WIBs. Lucy clucked her tongue, watching as a single rocket screamed into the night sky and exploded in a burst of light—a blossom of fiery sparks that bloomed and faded.

Soon the sky was filled with exploding fireworks, and the party moved to the upper deck, crowding around the railing facing the harbor.

Sue woke and, guessing that her greenish pallor was not the reflection of the fireworks, Lucy helped her up and led her downstairs. Unsure where the head was located, Lucy steered her toward the railing, just in case.

"Don' fee-el goo'," said Sue.

"Look at the fireworks," Lucy urged, hoping to distract her.

Sue clutched the railing and leaned over. Here we go, thought Lucy, but she was wrong. Sue was pointing to the water.

"Whaash tha?"

Lucy looked down and saw something white.

"A reflection?"

"No." Sue leaned over farther and Lucy grabbed the back of her dress.

"Whoa, there. You're going to fall in."

"Thas wha' happened. Somebody fell in."

Lucy looked again. Sue was right. Whatever was floating there did resemble a human shape.

"It's probably garbage or something," said Lucy, looking up as a giant rocket exploded overhead, filling the sky with light. In the distance she heard a boat motor start up, and she felt the yacht rock slightly under her feet as the wake hit.

"Not garbage." Sue tugged her sleeve. "Look."

Lucy looked and saw the white form now had arms and legs and a head, all floating a few inches below the surface of the water. Another wave came and the body rolled over. Even in the dim light, Lucy was sure it was Ron. The recognition hit her like a tidal wave, and she found herself gripping the railing with every bit of her strength.

Sue moaned. "I'm gonna be sick."

Chapter Thirteen

Lucy forced herself to unclench her hand and wrapped an arm around Sue, who promptly retched and heaved over the side. For a moment, everything receded to a distant point while she struggled to overcome her own queasiness. She set her teeth, took slow, steady breaths, and locked her gaze on to the beam of light streaming from the lighthouse on the point.

"Does the lady need some assistance?" inquired one of the stewards.

Lucy had never been so glad to see anyone in her life.

"Oh, yes," she said, pointing to the water. "There's a body."

The steward leaned over the rail, then snapped upright as if he had received a jolt of electricity.

"Don't move," he said. "I'll get help."

Lucy tightened her grip on Sue, who was bent over the railing and moaning, and started to count. She had gotten to twenty-seven when the steward returned with a splendidly uniformed man, whom Lucy took to be the captain, and a couple of crewmen. The steward hustled Sue off to a cabin, the captain ordered the crewmen into a small boat to check the body, and Lucy was led to a chair.

"What happened?" demanded the captain, keeping his voice low.

"We were watching the fireworks and my friend felt sick. We went to the back of the boat and there he was." Lucy bit her lip. "I think it's Ron Davitz."

One of the crewmen returned and whispered something in the captain's ear.

"Not a word to anyone," cautioned the captain. "I'm calling the police and confining the party to the grand saloon."

"What about me?" Lucy asked.

"You will stay where you are." He nodded at the crewman, who took a position behind her chair.

Lucy obeyed, waiting while the captain made a brief announcement and crew members ushered the group of women inside. She thought of Thelma and Sidra, still unaware of the terrible news they would soon hear. She thought of Sue, sick and alone belowdecks.

"Can't I go to my friend?" she asked the crewman.

"Sorry. Captain's orders."

The boat rocked slightly, and she thought of the body floating against the side of the boat. Ron's body.

"Is he still in the water?" she asked.

"Captain's orders were to remove him only if there were signs of life."

"Were there?"

He shook his head.

Lucy looked at him more closely and saw that he was no older than Toby. It was then that tears sprang to her eyes and she started to shake with sobs. The crewman put a hand on her shoulder and handed her a tissue. She sat there miserably, dabbing at her eyes, waiting for the police.

The last of the fireworks had fizzled to ashes, and only a few stragglers remained in the parking lot when the police arrived quietly, without sirens or flashing lights. Lucy, lost in her own thoughts, wasn't even aware they were on the scene until she was told the lieutenant wanted to talk to her and was ushered to a cabin.

As she expected, it was Lieutenant Horowitz. He was with the state police and responsible for investigating serious crimes in the area. Lucy and he had crossed paths many times before.

"Mrs. Stone," said the lieutenant, greeting her with his usual sad expression, "please sit down."

Lucy perched on the end of a bunk. The lieutenant was sitting only a few feet away in the tiny cabin, at a small desk that was mounted on the wall. They were so close that she couldn't avoid his gray eyes. She saw there was a poppy seed stuck between his teeth.

"Just start at the beginning," he said.

Lucy looked at her lap. When, exactly, was the beginning, she wondered. What incident had started the chain of events that had resulted in Ron's death? She looked at Horowitz blankly, noticing that the ceiling light glinted on the stubble that was reasserting itself on his clean-shaven chin.

"This was some sort of party?" he prompted.

"A wedding shower for Sidra Finch. She's engaged to Ron Davitz. He and his mother are visiting on this yacht to plan the wedding."

"When did you get here?"

"Seven, maybe."

"Did you notice anything out of the ordinary?"

"It was just a typical party. . . ."

Horowitz interrupted. "You call this typical? You go to a lot of parties on million-dollar yachts?"

"Ron's quite wealthy. He's supposed to be the next Bill Gates."

Horowitz raised his eyebrows.

"Like I said, it was a wedding shower. There were food and drinks. Sidra opened presents and then everybody went to the upper deck to see the fireworks."

"That's when you noticed the body?"

She nodded. "My friend, Sue Finch, Sidra's mother, had a little too much to drink. She felt sick so we moved away from the others, down to the lower deck. That's when we saw the body." Lucy paused. "Is it Ron?"

"The body hasn't been identified yet." Horowitz scratched his long upper lip. "Did you hear any splashes, an altercation, anything like that?"

Lucy took a sharp little breath. She remembered Sue telling her about Sid's gun. Could Ron have been shot? Could Sid have done it?

"Was he shot?" she asked.

Horowitz looked at her closely. "Did you hear a shot?"

"There were fireworks," she said.

"Yes." Horowitz's face was expressionless.

Lucy had to know. "Do you think he was shot?"

"I told you, we haven't recovered the victim yet."

"You said 'victim.' Does that mean it's homicide?"

"I don't know if he's a homicide victim or an accident victim. Right now, we've got a victim victim." Horowitz narrowed his eyes. "Is there something you're not telling me?"

"No." Lucy shook her head. From far off, she heard the rumble of thunder.

"I hope you're telling the truth."

"I am." She nodded.

He looked at her skeptically. "And you're going to leave this investigation to the police, right?"

"Of course." She pursed her lips. "Can I see Sue now?"

"Not until I've questioned her. Do you have your car here?"

"Yes."

"Can you drive?"

She nodded.

"Then I think you should go home."

"Home?" Lucy was dumbfounded. Everything was all

right at home. She was needed here. She couldn't leave Sue and Sidra. And what about Thelma? All three survivors would need sympathy and support. "They need me here."

"They're in good hands. Trust me." He opened the door and nodded at the uniformed trooper outside.

Lucy realized with a shock that she'd been under guard the whole time. Was she a suspect, or was this just standard crime scene procedure?

"Good night, Mrs. Stone."

She nodded mutely and followed the trooper off the boat and out to the parking lot, where a flash of lightning illuminated the scattered cars.

"Will you be all right? Do you want an escort?" asked the trooper. Lucy could hardly hear him over a thunderclap.

"I'll be okay," said Lucy, opening the door. But as she started the car, she realized that she was definitely not okay. Her emotions were a confused jumble of horror and anger and, most of all, fear. She was terrified of the revelations tomorrow might bring.

She shifted into gear and drove off as the first raindrops started to fall.

Chapter Fourteen

Maybe it was a dream—a nightmare—thought Lucy, as she drove through the downpour along the dark and empty roads that led home. Occasional flashes of lightning revealed familiar landmarks: Main Street turned into Main Street Extension; there was the stop sign at the intersection with Route One, and then the familiar turnoff onto Red Top Road. Nothing had changed. The Methodist Church was still standing on the corner of Main Street and Church Street; the Quik-Stop was in its usual place on Route One; there was still that dip in the road just before she began the climb up old Red Top Hill.

And when she got to the old farmhouse on top of the hill, the porch light would be on for her. Inside, Bill would probably be watching TV and the girls would be getting ready for bed or squabbling over the phone or deciding what to wear tomorrow. When she pulled into the driveway, Kudo would bark and scratch at the door until somebody let him outside so he could greet her properly.

Ron's death hadn't changed her life, but it had changed everything for Sidra. Lucy could remember the very moment it had occurred to her that something could happen to Bill. They had only been married for a few weeks; she was walking home from work, eagerly anticipating their daily reunion. What would it be like, she had wondered, if he wasn't there? That tiny, evil thought mushroomed in her mind until she was running down the street, terrified that he'd been hit by a car or shot in a holdup or stricken with a fatal heart attack. She'd burst into the house and flung herself in his arms, sobbing hysterically with relief to find him sitting at the kitchen table doing a crossword puzzle.

For Sidra, however, there would be no strong arms to embrace her; there would be no laughter over her silly fears. For her, the unthinkable had come true. She had lost the man she loved. The joy of her anticipated wedding had vanished, leaving nothing but pain and loss. Love was risky, thought Lucy, putting aside her dislike of Ron. He was the one Sidra had pinned all her hopes and dreams for the future on, he was the one she had chosen. And now, like a gambler who bets his entire stake in a game of chance, she had lost it all in one spin of the wheel.

The only thing worse than losing your partner, thought Lucy, would be losing your child. It wasn't supposed to happen like that. In the natural order of things, parents died first, leaving their children to perpetuate their line. From the first pangs of labor to the bloody birth and on through the perils of childhood, mothers learned to keep their eyes fixed firmly on the future. They poured love into their babies along with every ounce of milk, and willingly sacrificed their own health and comfort for the sake of their little ones. Thelma had been just such a mother; Lucy was sure of it. Once she was widowed, Ron had become the entire focus of her existence, and now he was gone.

Lucy groaned aloud, forcing herself to look at the possibility that Ron's death hadn't been accidental. This was one train of thought she didn't want to ride to the end of the line, but since Sue had told her the gun was missing, she had to consider the possibility that Sid had found it and used it. That, thought Lucy, would have all the trappings of tragedy. Sidra would lose not only her lover but her father; Sue would lose her husband and possibly her daughter; and Sid would lose everything.

Not so fast, thought Lucy. Here she was creating a Shakespearean drama, and she didn't even know if Ron had been murdered. Maybe he just slipped off the boat and banged his head. It happened. It wasn't time to panic—not yet. Right now, the best approach would be to wait and see. There was no sense in jumping to conclusions.

On the other hand, Lucy thought as she pulled into the driveway, it wouldn't hurt to be prepared for the worst. She turned off the ignition and sat for a moment, looking at the glowing porch light. A shadow appeared at the door, which opened, and she heard Kudo barking. She opened the car door and he bounded through the rain, tail wagging. She waited for him to shake, then got out of the car and ran with him, dodging puddles, to the house.

Bill opened the door for her and she ran inside, throwing her arms around him and burying her head in his chest and sobbing.

"Whoa," he said, stepping back to catch his balance. "What's all this?"

Excited by this display of emotion, Kudo pranced around them, barking.

From the family room, they heard Zoe shriek, "Mom's home!" In a moment, Zoe herself had thrown her small body against Lucy, wrapping her arms around her hips. Sara stood in the doorway, looking as if she wished she weren't far too sophisticated to join in the group hug.

Struggling to gain control of herself, Lucy used Bill's shirt to wipe her eyes.

"What's the matter?" he asked.

Zoe was jumping up and down, still caught up in holiday excitement. "I'm a firecracker," she said.

"Shut up," said Sara. "Can't you see Mom's upset?"

Zoe stepped back and looked up at her mother's face. "Sorry," she whispered.

"It's okay." Lucy stroked her cheek. "You had your face painted."

"At the party. Sadie's Mom did it. They're stars, see. Just like on a firecracker."

"I hope there weren't any real firecrackers," said Lucy, chattering and shaking. "They're dangerous."

"You better sit down," said Bill, pulling out a chair for her. "Sara, get your mother a blanket or something. Zoe, maybe you should get yourself to bed."

Zoe's face crumpled.

"It's okay, honey. Come sit on my lap."

Lucy rested her cheek on Zoe's silky little head and held her close, breathing in her sweet little-girl scent.

"You smell good," said Lucy, sniffling. "Like sunshine and shampoo."

Bill handed her a small glass of brandy and draped the afghan around her shoulders.

"Thanks," said Lucy, giving him a weak smile. "This was some night." She paused, sipping at her drink. "Ron's dead."

Bill didn't recognize the name. "Who's Ron?"

"Sidra's fiancé," said Sara, in an everybody-knows-that tone of voice and rolling her eyes.

"That's terrible," said Bill, too shocked at the news to scold her for being fresh. "What was it? A car crash?"

"I was on the yacht, waiting for the fireworks to start, and I looked down and he was . . ." Lucy paused to blow her nose. She took a deep breath. "He was in the water."

"You think he drowned?" asked Bill.

Lucy shook her head. "I don't know." She shuddered, recalling the sight of Ron's lifeless body floating beneath the surface. "The police were there."

Zoe let out a big sigh and leaned her back against her mother's chest. She'd been waiting a long time to tell her mother about the party and wasn't going to be distracted. "Well, we had a fight at Sadie's house with the boys. They were going to light firecrackers and throw them at the girls but I went and told Mr. Orenstein and he took them away. And he told the boys that if they kept bothering us girls he wouldn't let them stay up to see the fireworks."

Lucy could just picture Zoe's righteous indignation as she tattled on the boys and the thought made her smile.

"Did you have a good time, too, Sara?"

"It was okay. I got a home run."

Lucy knew that a game of softball was a July Fourth tradition at the Orensteins' barbecue.

"That's great. How'd your father do?"

"I got a base hit," said Bill, yawning. "And I caught a few high flies when I was fielding. Not bad for an old man."

Lucy glanced at the clock.

"Gosh, it's almost ten. You girls better get to bed or you'll be too tired for day camp tomorrow."

"Do I have to?" whined Zoe.

"You have to," said Lucy, setting her down on her feet and giving her a little push toward the stairs. "I'll be up to kiss you good night in a few minutes."

Bill waited until they were gone, then he sat down next to her at the table and took her hand.

"I want the whole story," he said in a low voice. "Not the G version. Do the cops think he was killed?"

Lucy clasped his hand with both of hers, holding on tightly.

"I don't know what they think. They didn't tell me. But they sure acted like something was funny. They separated everybody, wouldn't let people talk to each other. Then they made me leave; they wouldn't even let me help. Poor Sue. And Sidra." Lucy dabbed at her eyes. "His mother was there. He was dead in the water and everybody was having a party at the same time."

"It's awful," said Bill.

"Have you ever seen a drowned person?"

He shook his head.

"Well, I hope you never do," said Lucy, getting to her feet. "I better make sure the girls are settling down."

Climbing up the stairs, Lucy felt as if she were struggling up Heartbreak Hill in the Boston Marathon. Her legs simply didn't want to work. She felt like sitting down right there and going to sleep. Instead, she grabbed the railing and hauled herself up.

Sara was already in bed, a book propped on her chest, pointedly ignoring her little roommate. Zoe was flitting around the colorful toys that littered the floor in her Warrior Princess pajamas. Where did she get the energy? wondered Lucy as she struggled to produce one-word sentences.

"Bed. Now."

"Xena doesn't go to bed until . . ."

"Her mother tells her to."

Zoe started to turn back the bedspread, then looked up at Lucy. "Are you sure?"

"Xena's going to be too tired tomorrow to battle evil unless she goes to sleep right this minute."

Exhausted by the effort of speaking, Lucy sat down on the side of the bed. She patted it and Zoe wriggled in between the sheets. Lucy bent down to kiss her, then started to go. Zoe grabbed her hand.

"Didn't he know how to swim?" she asked.

Lucy sat back down and sighed.

"I guess not."

"How come? Everybody I know can swim. I can swim all the way out to the float and back. I'm an advanced beginner."

"Good for you," said Lucy. "When you pass the test

they'll give you a card with a red cross on it and I'll put it up on the refrigerator for everybody to see."

"And Dad'll give me a dollar?"

Lucy smiled at Zoe, who was determined to assert her claim to this family custom. Whenever the kids passed on to the next level of swimming lessons, Bill rewarded them with a crisp new dollar bill.

"You bet."

"I'm tired," groaned Sara, putting down her book. "I want to go to sleep."

"Good night, sleep tight," said Lucy, turning out the light.

"Don't let the bed bugs bite!" Zoe finished the rhyme for her.

Lucy shut the door, wondering if Zoe would ever calm down and go to sleep. In fact, tired as she was, she wondered if she would be able to sleep, considering how tense she felt. She decided to take a warm, relaxing bath. When she finished, Bill was already in bed.

She climbed under the covers and snuggled beside him, resting her head on his chest and stroking his curly, springy beard.

"I take you for granted," she said. "You've been a good husband and a good father all these years. I love you."

Bill kissed her head and mumbled something.

"If anything happened to you, I don't know what I'd do," continued Lucy. "I'd be lost without you."

Bill snored.

Lucy turned on her side and pushed her back against him, spoon-style. Then she reached up and turned out the lamp.

Chapter Fifteen

Next morning, the sun shone brightly in a cloudless blue sky. Birds twittered in the trees, rambling roses bobbed on fences, and fish leapt in the pond. If Nature were grieved at the loss of one of her children, she seemed to be hiding it rather well. Only the weeping willow tree seemed to sorrow at the news on the car radio that the next Bill Gates, Ron Davitz, had died and police were investigating.

Lucy dropped the girls at camp and drove on to the Queen Vic, where she pulled up in the circular driveway to let Elizabeth out of the car. Andy Dorfman spotted her from the porch and gave a wave, then hurried up to her car.

"Have you heard the news?" he asked, eagerly.

"It's very sad," said Lucy.

"Well, one man's loss is another man's gain," said Dorfman, adding a little whistle.

"What do you mean?"

"I got his last interview," he said, stepping back and raising his arms. "I can see the headline now: 'Davitz's Last Words: The Final Interview.'"

"You're sick," said Lucy, shifting into gear and rolling down the driveway.

"That's pretty cold," observed Toby from the backseat.

But when they got to the harbor, Geoff met them with a big wave.

"Did you hear about Davitz?" he asked brightly.

"I found his body."

"Oh, sorry," said Geoff, rearranging his features into a serious expression. "That must've been a shock."

"It was awful," Lucy admitted.

Geoff looked at the ground for a moment, then shrugged. "Oh, well, life goes on."

Lucy watched for a moment as he strode off with Toby. There was definitely a bounce in his step that hadn't been there before.

At the *Pennysaver,* Ted was busy organizing coverage of Davitz's sudden death. "We'll have an obit, of course, and we'll need a bio listing his achievements. We can probably get that off the Secure.net web page. Of course, everybody will have that. What we've got that nobody else has is the hometown advantage. That's what I want you to write, Lucy. Something about the impact of his death on our town—especially his fiancé."

Lucy stared at him. "I can't believe this."

"Now, don't get all huffy," he said. "You can do this sensitively."

"You want me to take advantage of my friendship with Sue to intrude on her privacy to write about how her daughter is coping with an absolutely devastating loss?"

Ted looked embarrassed. "Well, if you put it that way . . ."

"You bet I'm putting it that way. And I'm not writing the story."

"Okay. You write the obit and I'll see what I can do with the reaction story."

"Maybe you should kill it. Did you think of that?"

"Not gonna kill it." He set his chin. "I'll be sensitive. Promise."

"I'm out of here," said Lucy, grabbing her bag and heading for the door.

"Good idea," said Ted. "Take a personal day. I know this must be difficult for you. Take all the time you need."

The door slammed.

"Just get me that obit by Tuesday!" he shouted.

Outside, Lucy stood on the sidewalk, wondering what to do with herself. Spotting her friend Police Officer Barney Culpepper directing traffic at the corner, she walked in his direction. He joined her on the curb.

"Beautiful day, isn't it?" he said, sniffing the air appreciatively.

Barney was a big man, and the gesture reminded Lucy of a bear emerging from its den after a long winter's nap.

"It's almost too nice," said Lucy. "Considering what happened last night, it ought to be gray and rainy."

"I s'pose you were there at the party," said Barney.

"I was."

"Terrible thing to happen. The groom turns up dead at the wedding shower." He shook his head. "How's the bride taking it?"

"I don't know. Horowitz wouldn't let me see her last night. I guess I'll head over there now and see if there's anything I can do."

He nodded. "Marge is making a lasagna. She's going to stop by this afternoon."

Marge was Barney's wife, who had recently been given a clean bill of health after undergoing chemotherapy for breast cancer.

"How's Marge feeling?"

"Great. Says the whole thing gave her a new attitude. Every day is a gift."

Lucy watched as Barney held up his hand and stepped off the curb, stopping traffic so that a family of tourists could cross the street. When they were safely on the other side, he rejoined her.

"I feel so badly for Sidra," said Lucy, continuing the conversation.

"Aw, she's young," said Barney. "She'll get over it."

Lucy didn't agree. In her experience, younger people had a harder time dealing with loss than older folks. She suspected it was because they simply didn't expect it and hadn't developed any strategies for coping.

"Maybe," Lucy said with a shrug. She didn't want to argue, especially since she was hoping Barney would share some information with her. "Any word yet on how he died?" she asked, keeping her voice casual.

The effort was lost on Barney, who had leaped off the curb and was blowing his whistle furiously at a convertible that hadn't slowed for the crosswalk. Lucy watched as he reprimanded the young driver, even going so far as to pull his citation book out of his pocket. In the end, he let the kid go with only a verbal warning.

"Kids," he muttered when he returned. "They're so busy listening to the radio, they can't be bothered reading the signs."

"They're reckless," agreed Lucy. "Never think anything can happen to them." She paused. "Do they know what the cause of death was yet?"

"Haven't heard anything," admitted Barney.

"Last night it seemed as if they were treating it as a homicide," said Lucy.

"That's standard procedure at all fatals these days. Sometimes what looks like an accident isn't, if you know what I mean," he said with a knowing expression.

"But as far as you know, they haven't decided if it was an accident or not?"

He looked at her sharply. "Is there something you're not telling me? Some reason you think it wasn't an accident?"

Lucy opened her eyes wide and held up her hands in protest. "No, no. I was just wondering, that's all. Seeing he was so young and all, it seems funny he would drown like that. I mean, there were lots of people around, and he could easily have swum to a boat or a dock."

"Didn't know how to swim."

Lucy's chin dropped. "He couldn't swim?" she asked, incredulous.

To her, swimming was something children learned naturally, like walking and talking. Living on the coast and among so many lakes and ponds, her kids had grown up spending most of the summer either in or on the water.

"His mom said she thought it was too dangerous. Never let him learn."

That sounded just like Thelma, thought Lucy. "Penny wise and pound foolish."

"You said it."

Barney tipped his hat and stepped back into the intersection, which definitely needed his attention. Traffic had backed up as drivers futilely waited for a break so they could turn left. It was so bad that Lucy decided to walk around to Sue's rather than cope with the stop-and-go traffic on Main Street.

It was funny, she thought as she stood on the front step and prepared to ring the bell. From the outside, the house looked just the same as always. The neat lawn was edged with a border of flowers, white curtains were blowing at the open windows, and geraniums were blooming in a crock by the door. It was enough to break your heart. Lucy rang the bell.

"Thanks for coming," said Sue when she opened the door.

"Of course I'd come."

"I know," said Sue, hugging her.

"How are you doing?" Lucy thought Sue looked as attractive as ever, dressed in a simple T-shirt and linen shorts, with not a hair out of place. The only hint that something was amiss was the fact that the only jewelry she was wearing was her wedding ring.

"I'm okay—the doctor gave me some tranquilizers."

"Hey, whatever works," said Lucy, following Sue to the kitchen. "How's Sidra?"

"Still asleep. It was late when we got home last night, after the police and everything. She went in her room and shut the door. I didn't sleep much myself and I checked on her a few times, but she was always sound asleep."

"That's all for the best, I guess," said Lucy, taking a seat at the table.

"Coffee?"

"No, thanks," said Lucy, thinking that the house was awfully quiet. In Tinker's Cove, friends and relatives usually rallied around following a death. Family members gathered to tend to the needs of the bereaved, the phone rang off the hook with offers to help, and a steady stream of visitors brought baked goods and casseroles. Florists' trucks arrived regularly with arrangements, and the mailbox was full of sympathy cards. "I saw Barney on the way over. He said Marge was making lasagna for you."

"Bless her."

"Has anyone else called?"

"Don't know." Sue was looking out the window. "I turned off the phone. I didn't want the ringing to bother Sidra."

"Oh. I didn't know you could do that."

"Sure."

"And where's Sid? Did he go to work?"

"Uh, no. He's away."

Lucy was shocked. "Away?"

"He left yesterday. He wanted to avoid the shower and all that, so he went fishing for a few days."

"Ah." Lucy couldn't help thinking it was a good thing Sid had an alibi, just in case Ron's death wasn't accidental.

"You know what Barney told me? He said Thelma

told the police she never let him learn to swim. Can you believe it?"

Sue pounced on the news. "He drowned?" she asked. "Is that what the police say?"

"They don't know yet." Lucy hated to disappoint her, especially since it seemed those tranquilizers weren't working too well. Sue was obviously as tense as a mother cat watching the family dog sniffing at her kittens. "Barney did say that they investigate all sudden deaths the same way. Just because Horowitz was questioning everybody last night doesn't mean they think it's a murder or anything."

"That's good." Sue seemed to relax a little. "Coffee?"

"You already asked me. I don't want any, but go ahead and have some if you want it."

"I think I will." Sue poured herself a mugful and brought it over to the table, where she sat down next to Lucy.

She didn't say anything, and the silence hung awkwardly between them. Finally, thinking over the events of the previous night, Lucy remembered the WIBs.

"What happened to the bridesmaids?" she asked. "Are they staying here?"

Sue's head snapped around to confront her. "Don't ask me. I didn't invite them—they're not my responsibility." She sipped her coffee. "They're Thelma's guests and she can take care of them."

"Of course," said Lucy, reminding herself that she shouldn't judge Sue. She had never had to cope with anything like this, and she didn't really know what she would do. "Poor Thelma. She must be devastated."

"Poor Thelma! She's got the entire staff of that yacht to take care of her, and I'm willing to bet she's making sure they do. I'm not worried about Thelma. The one I'm worried about is Sidra."

"Of course," said Lucy, gently. "But you have some responsibility for Thelma, too. After all, you almost became family."

"It was a close call," said Sue with a sardonic little chuckle.

Appalled, Lucy drew back in her chair.

"Don't act so shocked, Lucy. It's not as if you like her any more than I do. She's awful and so was Ron. I'm not afraid to say it: I'm glad he's dead. I never liked him; I never thought he was the right man for Sidra. She was making a horrible mistake marrying him, and now . . ."

"Mother!"

Sidra, pale and disheveled, was standing in the door-way, dressed in what Lucy suspected was her wedding-night lingerie. She stayed there for a moment, swaying on her feet, and then turned and ran down the hall, sobbing.

"Oh, shit," said Sue, jumping to her feet and hurrying after her.

Left alone in the kitchen, Lucy decided this was a good time to leave. She was closing the door after her when a long, white stretch limousine pulled up at the curb. A black-tinted window slid open and Norah Hemmings poked her head out.

"Lucy! Come here!" ordered the queen of daytime TV. "I want to talk to you."

"Hi," said Lucy, bending awkwardly down to the window.

"Never mind that; come on in here. We'll go for a lit-tle spin."

Lucy pulled the door open and climbed in beside Norah, who was surrounded with a clutter of papers and a laptop computer.

"How is Sidra?" she demanded as the car glided along. "I flew up as soon as I heard."

Lucy thought of the distressing scene she had just wit-nessed. "She needs time," she finally said, relaxing on the cushioned seat and enjoying the air-conditioning. "I'd give her some time before you go back."

"The poor child. I suppose she's sobbing her heart out."

Lucy nodded.

"I just know she's heartbroken, poor thing. And her parents must be so upset, too." Norah expelled a sharp little breath. "It's just tragic, absolutely tragic. So young, the whole future ahead of them, and poof, it's all over before it started. I just don't think I can stand it."

"It's horrible," agreed Lucy. "Especially for his mother."

"That's right. His mother's here, too." Norah paused, and Lucy could have sworn she heard a Rolodex spinning in her head. "Thelma?"

"Thelma."

"Ahh, Thelma. An interesting woman."

"You've met her?"

"Several times. At benefits and things." Norah paused and smoothed her skirt. "And Ron, too, of course."

"The next Bill Gates."

"So they said." Norah looked out the window at the stately captain's homes they were passing, each set well back from the road, looking out on a spacious lawn dotted with big, old trees. Even a few mulberry trees, living relics of the China trade. "You know what these houses say to me? They say they were built by daring men who made their fortunes by sailing around the world, risking their lives to bring back goods and merchandise. Real stuff: lumber or bricks or dishes or tea. Something real, something you could weigh and measure and stock in a warehouse. It's different nowadays. This Internet is just a lot of electrical impulses or something, and people are getting rich from it. I don't understand it at all."

"I don't either," admitted Lucy. "But you can't argue with success. Ron was doing something right; they say he was a genius."

"That may be so, but frankly, I never understood what Sidra saw in him." Norah placed a hand on Lucy's arm and leaned closer. "You know, I interview all sorts of people on my TV show, and after a while, you develop a sense about people. Whether they're genuine or not, you know."

Norah tapped her finger against Lucy's arm. "There was something about him that just didn't ring true, if you ask me." She sighed. "It was the other fellow I really liked. Now, what was his name? Greg? Something like that."

Lucy made a guess. "You don't mean Geoff Rumford?"

Norah's face lit up. "That was it! I only met him once, but I used to see him around the studio quite a lot. Waiting for her after work, you know, and she always seemed happy to see him. Frankly, I was quite surprised when she started going out with Ron."

Lucy was philosophical. "I suppose it would be hard for someone like Geoff to compete with the next Bill Gates."

Norah looked at her. "I never thought Sidra was a gold digger."

"I didn't mean that, exactly. But the fact remains that Geoff's a struggling grad student. He probably couldn't afford to take her to the movies. And a girl can get pretty tired of walks in the park and spaghetti suppers," said Lucy. "You can drop me here—my car's just ahead."

"It's nice seeing you—and being back in Tinker's Cove. So normal. Not like New York. Lance is with me, you know. I'm sure he'll be looking for Elizabeth."

"She's working at the Queen Vic this summer, saving for college."

"See what I mean? This town is so wholesome."

Lucy looked up and down Main Street, where the red, white, and blue bunting still hung from the street lamps and the sidewalk was filled with vacationing families. Appearances can be deceiving, she thought as she opened the car door.

"Thanks for the lift," she said.

Chapter Sixteen

Lucy sat in her car for a minute, waiting for an opening in the Main Street traffic. A bumper sticker on a passing pickup caught her eye: "TINKER'S COVE: A QUAINT DRINKING VILLAGE WITH A FISHING PROBLEM."

The stickers had been a fad a couple of years ago, when the state first announced the lobster quota, and a human services report issued about the same time concluded the town had a higher rate of alcoholism than the rest of the state. As far as Lucy could tell, the stickers had faded and begun to curl around the edges, but the town still had the same problems: too few lobsters and too much drinking. Summer vacation was starting to seem very long, especially now that Toby had discovered the Bilge. There was plenty of time for him to get into trouble, she decided, counting the weeks until he would return to college.

Seeing a break, Lucy pulled out of her parking space and joined the line of traffic. She was behind a van from Maryland loaded down with a roof carrier and bicycles—a familiar sight in summer. She supposed the people in the van had the same view of Tinker's Cove that Norah did: a wholesome New England village.

A harbor filled with colorful boats, white clapboard houses, and window boxes filled with geraniums could sure give people the wrong impression, Lucy thought bitterly. Take Sue, for example. She lived in a charming house; she was planning her daughter's wedding; it all looked so perfect from the outside.

On the inside, however, it was a different story. What a tangle of emotions! Sidra had fallen in love with Ron, but Sue and Sid didn't approve. Now that Ron was dead, Sue was relieved but Sidra was broken-hearted. As for Sid, he was out of town, and Sue seemed in no hurry to have him return. You might almost think that Sue was worried Sid would be a suspect.

Lucy braked for the traffic light. If Sid was a suspect, so were plenty of other people, she thought. Geoff Rumford came to mind. As a jilted lover, he certainly had a motive. And there was no love lost between him and Ron. Lucy herself had seen the two men argue. Of course, the entire commercial fishing fleet also detested Ron, with his rented yacht and his buckets of money. Any one of them could have had a few too many beers at the Bilge and sent him off the end of the pier, especially if Ron had gotten into an argument over the parade float. Even Wiggins might have blamed Ron for subjecting him to the fishermen's ridicule.

The light changed and Lucy drove on slowly in the stop-and-go traffic that had become typical in summer. She thought of Dorfman—he certainly wasn't shedding any tears over Ron, but Lucy didn't think he would actually kill the man in order to get "The Final Interview." On the other hand, she had seen the two of them arguing at Jake's Donut Shack. Ron had certainly had a knack for ticking people off, and he might have pushed Andy Dorfman too far.

Finally breaking free of the downtown congestion, Lucy accelerated on Main Street Extension. A glance at the speedometer told her she was going fifteen miles above the speed limit, so she lifted her foot off the gas pedal. Whoa, she told herself, thinking that she ought to rein in her thoughts as well. She didn't even know for sure that Ron had been murdered. Maybe he just slipped and fell off the dock. What horrible irony that would be. Drowning within just a few feet of his yacht. All that money was absolutely no good to a man who'd fallen in the water and couldn't swim.

Lucy turned into the driveway and was greeted by Kudo, who ran up to the car with his tail wagging. She started walking to the house, but he didn't follow her as he usually did. He stood in the yard grinning, showing his white teeth and pink tongue.

"What do you want?" she asked.

He turned and headed for the dirt road leading to Blueberry Pond that ran behind their property.

"You want a walk?" Lucy asked. "Maybe a swim?" It sounded fine to her.

Seeing her following him, Kudo showed his approval by running back and forth and wagging his tail furiously. Lucy couldn't help smiling at this display of doggy enthusiasm, but she had to admit that, while the walk was a distraction, it wasn't a solution.

What was really bothering her? she wondered. Was she really that upset by Ron's death? It was undeniably tragic— a young man with so much potential lost—but Lucy couldn't truthfully say that she grieved for Ron. It was horrible for the women who loved him, of course. She would have to pay a visit to Thelma, she realized, but not just yet. And her heart went out to Sidra, but from what she'd seen at the shower, Sidra wasn't quite the sweet, sensitive girl she remembered. Furthermore, there was the niggling doubt whether Sidra had really loved Ron, even if she had managed to convince herself that she did.

It was none of those things, thought Lucy as she stepped out into the clearing and saw the sparkling

blue water of the pond. Kudo was involved in his favorite game of chasing the tadpoles that lined the
water's edge, but his antics didn't make her smile. She
stepped from rock to rock, finally perching on a big
boulder. There, she took off her shoes and let her feet
dangle into the pond. The cool water felt delicious. She
took a deep breath and relaxed, pressing her back
against the sun-warmed rock.

She was depressed, she realized, recognizing the
black cloud that had settled on her heart. And she knew
why. In the past, she'd always been able to share her
thoughts and fears with Sue. But now, all these walls
that Sue was busily building in an effort to avoid facing
the truth had created a barrier between them. In all the
years they had been friends, Lucy had never before felt
shut out. But now she was.

Sue had become so defensive and guarded that conversation didn't flow; it was like walking on a minefield.
Lucy never knew when she would say the wrong thing
and Sue would close up. Lucy understood that her
friend was unhappy—the wedding hadn't gone the way
she wanted; Ron was behaving strangely; Sidra had disappointed her. But before, Sue wouldn't have dealt with
these problems by drinking too much; she wouldn't
have started popping tranquilizers. She would have had
a heart-to-heart chat with Lucy.

Oh, she'd been chatting, thought Lucy, kicking her
feet in the water. But she had only been going through
the motions. There was something Sue was keeping
from her—something Sue didn't want to share—and it
made her feel sad. She shared everything with Sue; why
couldn't Sue do the same with her? What secret could
her friend possibly have that was so terrible she couldn't
share it?

Oh my God! thought Lucy, sitting bolt upright. What if
Sue had killed Ron? That would explain everything.
Her drunkenness at the shower. Her tension. Her odd

little silences. Her decision to sequester herself, unwilling to accept her friends' attention and condolences.

Lucy was on her feet. She jumped off the rock and started pacing back and forth on the gravelly beach. She couldn't be still; she had to move. *It can't be true, it can't be true,* she muttered as she headed back for the path. Sue would never do such a thing. Never.

Sid, she was willing to admit, had a tendency to go a bit too far in defense of his family. Lucy could remember an incident when Sidra was involved in a minor automobile accident and Sid had marched into the emergency room and confronted the motorist who had rear-ended her car. And there was the time at the pizza place when Sid hadn't liked the way a customer was looking at Sidra and had threatened him. Sid was a little hotheaded, but not Sue.

Sue was calm and rational, thought Lucy, striding back to the house. She was warm and nurturing and . . . Lucy stopped dead in her tracks. She could remember it as clearly as if it had been yesterday. Sue had called, absolutely mortified. Sidra was in eighth grade and for some reason or other hadn't made the honor roll. Sue confessed she had gone into the principal's office and completely lost her temper. In fact, Lucy remembered, Sue had been so embarrassed that she'd resigned as class mother and avoided the school until the man left to take a new job a year later.

Lucy was standing there, lost in her thoughts, when Kudo trotted up and, planting his feet firmly on the path, gave himself a good shake and Lucy a cold shower in the process.

"Thanks, I needed that," she told him as they continued along the path. She felt, she realized, like Marge must have felt when she'd gone for a routine mammogram and learned that there was a suspicious lump. There was nothing to do then, Marge had told her, but to hope for the best while preparing for the worst.

That was what she was going to have to do, too. Now that the possibility that Sue might have killed Ron had reared its ugly head, she was going to have to face it and find out if it was true. But first, she realized, glancing at the clock as she stood at the kitchen sink and drank a glass of water, she had to pick up the kids.

Lucy got to the Queen Vic a few minutes before five. She sat in the car, waiting for Elizabeth. Waiting, she thought, was about all she was up to. After all the emotions of the afternoon, she felt completely spent.

"That Mrs. McNaughton is so unfair," exclaimed Elizabeth, yanking the car door open and startling her.

"Hi, Elizabeth," she responded, with a deliberate show of manners, "it's nice to see you. Did you have a nice day?"

The subtle lesson was lost on Elizabeth, who plopped herself down in the passenger seat.

"Nice day? Are you kidding? I mean, even when it's a normal day, it's disgusting. I'm a chambermaid, for Pete's sake. And today was not normal. That writer guy, the one in 3B, Dorfman, complained to Mrs. McNaughton that his notes and tapes were missing, and of course, she accused me. Which is so stupid, because what would I want with that stuff anyway? Besides, that guy is such a pig, it's probably all there but he just can't find it. Like it's my fault if I have to move his stuff around just to make the bed and dust the room. But I wouldn't steal it—give me a break here."

Lucy resisted the urge to giggle hysterically. Elizabeth, who was affectionately known as "Piggy" at home, did not see the irony of the situation.

"I don't think you're even listening to me," complained Elizabeth. "Can't you say something?"

"I'm sorry," said Lucy. "I'm a little upset. I've been thinking about Ron's death and all."

"Yeah, that is weird, isn't it? They say he just fell in the water and drowned, right next to his boat. You'd think he would have yelled or something."

Elizabeth's casual comment hit Lucy like a punch to the stomach. Of course he would have yelled—if he'd just slipped into the water accidentally. But all those people on the yacht hadn't heard a thing.

"I don't think they know for sure how he died," she said, wondering if the music and talk had been loud enough to cover the cries of a desperate man.

"It's creepy. One minute he was alive, and the next he was dead." Elizabeth pondered this conundrum for a moment. "You know, I saw him yesterday. Right here in the inn."

Lucy was interested. "When was this?"

"Sometime in the afternoon. Kind of late, I think. Just before I left."

"Around four or five?"

"I think so. Why are you so interested?"

"Like you said, he was alive and then he was dead. I was wondering what he was doing before he died."

"Well, when I saw him, he was coming down the stairs from the third floor."

"That's the floor Dorfman's room is on?"

"Yeah." Elizabeth stared out the window for a minute. "This is really crummy for Sidra, isn't it?"

"It's awful."

"She was planning her wedding. . . ."

Lucy responded with a sniffle.

"So, what do you do when this happens?" demanded Elizabeth. "I mean, do you get to keep the ring? What about your wedding dress? Can you return it and get all your money back? And the shower presents—can she keep them? I heard she got quite a haul."

"Elizabeth," Lucy exclaimed, losing patience. "This isn't like your prom date changed his mind or something. Ron's dead. Sidra's lost the man she loves. It's tragic. Somehow, I don't think she's even thinking about the dress or the presents."

"I suppose not," said a chastened Elizabeth.

Lucy turned onto Sea Street and back to the harbor to pick up Toby. The parking lot was full of boxy trucks with satellite dishes on top; Ron's death would make the TV newscasts this evening. A lone police cruiser remained at the yacht, probably to keep the reporters from bothering Thelma. Lucy parked nearby, as close as she could get to the pier.

"Do you think Ron could have been visiting Dorfman?" she asked.

"Probably," said Elizabeth. "After all, Dorfman is doing a story on him. Most of the stuff in his room is about Ron." She gasped. "You don't think Ron took the tapes and stuff, do you? Maybe he didn't like the way the story was going or something."

"It's something to think about," said Lucy. She gazed out over the harbor, looking for the Lady L. "You know who I saw today? Norah."

"Oh," said Elizabeth.

"She said Lance is here with her."

"That's interesting," Elizabeth said in a carefully neutral voice.

"I thought you'd be more excited. I thought you and he kind of have a thing, maybe, sort of. You know."

"He's okay, but he's so immature. And I'm not going to be able to see much of him, anyway, since I'm working. I can't spend my time lying around the pool or riding a jet ski like he can."

"You make it sound as if you're in a penal colony. You do have days off, you know."

"I'm volunteering to help with the lobster project on my days off," Elizabeth said, surprising her. "I thought it would be good for college."

Lucy nodded, not quite sure what to think. Maybe Elizabeth was interested in turning over a new leaf, or maybe she had come up with a way of getting closer to Geoff.

Seeing Toby approaching the dock in a dinghy, Lucy honked her horn and checked her watch. Once again, she was going to be late picking up Zoe and Sara.

Chapter Seventeen

It was the top story on the local TV news Friday night: Ron Davitz's death had been ruled a homicide by the medical examiner. Autopsy results had revealed there was no water in Davitz's lungs, which meant he had been dead when he hit the water. Further examination had revealed bruising and lacerations consistent with a blow to the head. The time of death had not yet been determined.

"I wonder how they can be so sure it was a homicide," said Lucy. "Maybe he hit his head accidentally on something on his way into the water."

She and Bill were sitting together in the family room, drinking their after-dinner coffee and catching up on the day's news.

"It's amazing what these forensic guys can figure out just from the body," said Bill.

"I'm so glad he wasn't shot."

"What do you mean? What does it matter how he was killed?"

"Because," said Lucy, "Sue found a gun in the house, and considering how much Sid disliked Ron, it seemed possible he might have shot him."

"Sid?" snorted Bill. "That's crazy."

"Not so crazy, especially since he's left town."

"The man went fishing. He goes this time every year."

Lucy didn't like Bill's tone.

"Well, it did seem pretty suspicious," said Lucy, defending her thinking. "Especially with the wedding coming up. But now that Ron wasn't shot, it couldn't have been Sid."

"I don't follow your logic at all," said Bill, leaning back in the recliner and opening the sports section of the paper. "Sid could have hit him on the head with the gun."

Lucy's jaw dropped. "You think Sid did it!"

"No, I don't." Bill lowered the paper. "If you ask me, I think it's unlikely his death had anything to do with Tinker's Cove. This guy had connections all over the world, and you know what they say, you don't get to be that rich without stepping on a few toes." Bill narrowed his eyes. "Lucy, you're not getting involved in this thing, are you?"

"Of course I'm involved. Sue's my best friend. I work for the newspaper. How can I not be involved?"

"You know what I mean, Lucy. You're not conducting a private little investigation of your own, are you? Because if you've got time for something like that, you could be taking care of some things around here." He disappeared behind the paper.

"What, exactly, do you think I've been neglecting around here? You've got clean clothes; the house is relatively clean; you get a hot meal every night."

"Well, if you don't see what's wrong, there's no point talking about it. We'd just fight."

"So we're going to play Twenty Questions instead of discussing this like mature people?"

Bill's only reply was to turn a page of the paper.

Disgusted, Lucy picked up her coffee and carried it out to the gazebo. Sometimes the man could be so infuriating. What was going on? Okay, she hadn't asked his permission for the wedding; well, there wasn't going to be a wedding now. And so far, she'd been covering all the bases despite working extra hours. The girls were enjoying summer camp; Elizabeth and Toby were getting to work on time; the house was running pretty much as usual. What did he have to complain about?

She sat there, looking out at the distant mountains, wondering what to do. Bill did have a point: she had been accused often enough of poking her nose into police investigations and muddling up the evidence. Lt. Horowitz had threatened more than once to charge her with obstructing an investigation.

But this time, she didn't have a choice. Ron's murder was a big story and Ted would expect her to help cover it. Furthermore, her best friend and her family were directly involved. She couldn't pretend the whole thing wasn't happening, she thought, glumly resting her chin on her hand. Kudo settled down beside her and she idly scratched the top of his head. If only she could be as certain as Bill that Sid wasn't the murderer.

Come to think of it, she realized, Bill could have been on to something when he'd said Ron's death probably had nothing to do with Tinker's Cove. She had been foolish to think that, just because Davitz had died in Tinker's Cove, that meant the primary suspects had to be locals. That wasn't necessarily the case, considering that Ron had been such an important businessman. He had only been visiting in Tinker's Cove; he didn't live here. He would naturally have a wide circle of friends and acquaintances and business contacts stretching far beyond this little town.

There were, for instance, the muscle-bound men in white polo shirts she'd seen at the coffee shop. They had definitely been interested in Davitz. Who were they, she wondered. She had assumed they were bodyguards, but could they have been hired killers? She had to write an obit anyway; she might as well do a little extra research and see what she could turn up about Davitz and his possible enemies. She swallowed the last of her coffee and stood up.

But what, she asked herself as she paused to examine the tomato plants in her garden, would she do if she discovered that Sid, or even Sue, had really killed Davitz? Not intentionally, of course. She didn't think either one was capable of planning a murder. But what if there had been an argument that led to a fatal blow? What would she do then?

Noticing nothing but a stem where a leaf used to be, Lucy looked closer and spotted a plump tomato hornworm industriously munching his way along another leaf. In its way, with its bright green body and black-and-cream stripes and spots, it was a magnificent creature, and for a second she was tempted to leave it alone. Then she remembered the damage a single hornworm could do to an entire bed of tomato plants and plucked it off, dropped it on the ground, and stepped on it.

Remembering her instructions from Ted, Lucy spent several hours over the weekend on the Internet, researching Ron Davitz. Although she turned up plenty of information for the obit she had been assigned to write, she didn't come up with anything that would suggest he had enemies in the business world.

She also called Sue several times with offers of help but was politely rebuffed.

"Thanks, Lucy, but we're doing fine," was all Sue would say.

From Elizabeth, who had changed her mind about spending time with Lance, she learned that Norah had taken Thelma under her wing. She'd also invited the bridesmaids to stay with her at her enormous summer "cottage" on Smith Heights Road.

On Monday she hurried into work, eager for the latest news on the police investigation.

Ted shook his head. "Nothing, nada, zip. No press conferences, not even a statement." He paused. "Did you do the obit?"

Lucy gave him the floppy disk and sat down at her desk, where an enormous pile of press releases awaited her attention. It was almost lunchtime, and she was deeply immersed in the details of a silent auction when Ted got around to editing the obit.

"Nice work," he said after reading it. "You did a good job of explaining what Secure.net actually does."

"I'm not sure I really understand it," Lucy confessed, "but greater minds than mine seem to think it's the greatest thing since sliced bread. Do you know the stock was initially offered at twenty-five dollars a share, rose to forty-seven, and settled at forty-two dollars on the first day of trading? They say Ron made millions in that one day alone."

Ted shook his head. "Do you have the feeling that we're missing the party? People are making fortunes in the stock market, and I can't even fund my IRA to get the tax break."

"I've got a mutual fund," said Phyllis.

Ted and Lucy were impressed.

"How's it doing?" asked Ted. "Are you going to be retiring soon?"

"Not likely. It's been losing money."

Lucy was surprised. "Losing? I thought everyone was making money."

"Everyone but me," said Phyllis, watching as Lucy took a tin out of her tote bag. "Are those homemade cookies?"

Lucy peeked inside, then closed the lid. "Sorry. I'm taking them to Thelma."

"You are an angel," said Phyllis.

"Want to come with me?"

"Uh, I would," began Phyllis, "but I'm spending my lunch hour at the beach."

Lucy chuckled. "I'll pass along your condolences," she said.

When she stepped out into the sunshine, Lucy was tempted to forget about visiting Thelma. It was a gorgeous summer day, and this was no way to spend her precious lunch hour. She sighed and headed for the harbor.

Passing the town hall, she met Chuck Swift, dressed in his working clothes of rubber overalls and heavy rubber boots.

"Aren't you warm in that getup?" she asked.

"You bet, but I was in a hurry. Came straight here from my boat."

"What's up?"

"Plenty," he said. "That check that Davitz gave the town for docking privileges is no good."

"How do you know?"

"My mom works in the town hall, you know. She told me. It kind of puts the waterways commission's policy on transients in a new light. A pretty questionable light, if you ask me, since town residents have to pay for the entire season in advance. And if your check bounces, you lose your slip. They give it to the next guy on the list."

"They didn't make Davitz pay in advance?"

"Nope. He just waved his checkbook and they couldn't do enough for him."

"So the town's out more than ten thousand dollars?"

"Closer to twenty now." He snorted. "And you know what's really crazy about this? With all the news coverage and all, they're not going to make the boat move, either. I just talked to Chairman Wiggins. He says they can't add to a grieving mother's distress. What do you think of that?"

"I think some people are going to be wearing egg on their faces for quite a while," said Lucy, chuckling. "But you know, this happens a lot with rich people. I've heard Dot at the IGA complaining about how those rich summer people on Smith Heights Road run up huge charges at the store and never seem to be in much of a hurry to pay their bills. I even heard the dry cleaner has cut off some of those people. Refuses to take their dirty clothes unless they pay up front."

"Maybe the waterways commission should do the same thing," suggested Chuck. "You can be sure the commercial fishermen's association is going to be out in force at the next meeting, and I think we can get some support from the taxpayers' association, too. Let's face it, nobody in this town gets away with paying taxes or fees late. You're late, the penalties start to mount, and pretty soon they've got a lien on your property."

"He only rented the yacht, so they can't exactly put a lien on it."

"Too bad." He cocked his head. "Say, where are you headed? I've got the truck around back. Can I give you a lift?"

"No, thanks. I can use the exercise. See you later."

When Lucy got to the yacht, she paused at the gangway. Without a doorbell or knocker, she wasn't sure how to announce herself. Maybe she should yell "Ahoy, there" or something.

Her steps on the rubber-coated sheet metal made quite a lot of noise, and when she stepped onto the boat she gave a yell.

"Hi, there."

Nobody answered.

She stood, holding her tin of cookies, and waited a few minutes. She knew the yacht had a huge staff. Sooner or later, someone would appear. There was no shade where she was standing, so she took a few steps farther until she was under an awning. She considered poking her head into the saloon, but decided against it. If Thelma was sitting there, grieving, she didn't want to burst upon her unannounced. She waited.

Still no one came. Finally, she decided a little walk around the deck might be in order. She would be sure to bump into a crew member then. A circuit of the lower deck revealed no one, however, so she decided to climb to the upper deck, where the bridge was located. Surely someone would be there.

Sure enough, as she drew closer to the bridge, she heard voices coming through the open windows.

". . . hell of a spot," she heard a male voice complain. "The company wants me to oust her and set sail for Boston tomorrow. They've got a late booking, wants to cruise the coast for two weeks. I asked them, what am I supposed to do with her?" He snorted. "They said to jettison her unless she comes up with some cash."

This was met with laughter from someone else, and Lucy thought this would be a good time to make herself known.

"Ahoy!" she called, feeling slightly ridiculous.

A member of the crew appeared at the door. "Can I help you?"

"I came to see Mrs. Davitz. Is she home—I mean, aboard?"

"Follow me," he said, taking Lucy back down to the lower deck and leading her through the grand saloon. As they passed through, Lucy noticed a large number of flower arrangements and fruit baskets. Continuing down a flight of stairs, the steward paused outside a closed door, knocked, and entered, leaving Lucy in the passage. In a moment, he returned and told her Mrs. Davitz would see her.

Lucy had expected the stateroom to be luxurious, but she hadn't expected it to be quite so spacious. Far away, across yards of white broadloom, Thelma was perched in a silk-covered easy chair, with a stack of letters in her lap.

Lucy hurried over to her, proffering her tin of cookies. "I just wanted to come and tell you how sorry I am," she said.

Deftly Thelma took the tin with one hand and used the other to clasp Lucy's hand.

"You are so sweet to think of me," she said, "in this terrible time."

Lucy extricated herself and sat in the companion chair, waiting while Thelma dabbed her eyes and composed herself.

"I'll never forgive myself," said Thelma, patting her gray twin set and rattling her ropes of pearls. "My last words to him were . . . unpleasant. We were arguing, about the shower. I so wanted him to come. He said he had better things to do." She sniffed. "Why couldn't I let it go?" She raised her eyes to meet Lucy's. "I never had a chance to say good-bye. But how are you supposed to know that you'll never see . . ."

Thelma bent her head, unable to go on, and Lucy passed her a box of tissues.

"You couldn't know," said Lucy, in a soothing voice. She waited while Thelma dried her eyes. "I see you've gotten a lot of flowers—a lot of people are going to miss Ron very much."

Thelma sighed. "People have been so kind. See this phalaenopsis orchid? Barbara Walters sent it. And this one, it's from Diane Sawyer and Mike Nichols. That fruit basket, it's from Gwyneth Paltrow—such a dear. And, of course, Norah's been an absolute wonder. I would never have been able to get through the last few days without her."

Lucy wondered if Thelma knew that her time on the yacht was running out. "Maybe you should stay with her for a while," she suggested. "You'd be a lot more comfortable at her place, and you wouldn't be alone."

"I really am alone, aren't I?" Thelma sniffed. "I've lost my husband, and now my only child is gone, too."

"It's terrible, I know," said Lucy. "Can I get you something? Some tea? Would you like a piece of candy?"

Thelma dabbed at her eyes. "I think I could manage one of those Godiva chocolates."

Lucy followed her pudgy, beringed finger and saw a stack of candy boxes on a table. She went over and opened the top one.

"No, dear. The Godivas are in the gold box."

Lucy found the box and carried it over to Thelma, who studied the contents.

"None of them look very appealing," she said.

Lucy couldn't agree and hoped Thelma would offer her one. After all, she hadn't had lunch yet.

"I guess I'll try this one." Thelma plucked a dark chocolate heart out of the box and slowly placed it in her mouth. Then she put the lid back on the box and set it on the table next to her.

"Have you made any plans for a funeral service?" inquired Lucy.

"I'm waiting to hear from Ron's company," said Thelma, reaching for another chocolate. "I've put in several calls, but they haven't called back."

"No one has called back?" Lucy thought this was odd.

"No." Thelma was looking in the box, trying to decide which to eat next. "I suppose they're discussing what sort of observance would be most suitable. Perhaps they will have him lie in state in the company headquarters."

Lucy thought this was unlikely. "Where are the company headquarters?"

Thelma looked rather blank. "I don't actually know. Isn't that funny?"

Pretty funny, thought Lucy. "I suppose a lot of men keep their business lives separate from their private lives."

Thelma nodded, her mouth too full to answer until she swallowed. "Ron was just like that. He was absolutely fierce about it. Never let me so much as peek in his briefcase." Thelma sighed. "But I can't really complain. He was very generous to me. He was a wonderful son."

Lucy nodded sympathetically. "You must have so

many wonderful memories of him," she said. "No one can take those from you. You will always have them to take comfort from." Lucy hesitated, then continued. "I wonder, what is your last memory of Ron?"

Thelma sucked on a chocolate and leaned her head back, apparently searching her memory.

"He went off to town around five o'clock. For a meeting with that writer from *CyberWorld* magazine, he said. I've already told you I was upset with him, seeing we were going to have the shower so soon." She dabbed at her eyes. "I didn't see him after that." Thelma looked at her. "You never know, do you? When you say good-bye to someone, it may be for the very last time."

"You never know," Lucy agreed, thinking that if Thelma was correct, Dorfman was probably the last one to see Ron alive. Had there been some sort of confrontation about the missing notes? She stood up to go.

"Oh, do you have to leave so soon?" Thelma was disappointed.

"I'm afraid so."

"I understand," she answered, in a resigned voice. "Would you please pass me that basket of fruit?"

Chapter Eighteen

People's reactions to death were never quite what you expected, Lucy thought, reminding herself that it wasn't fair to judge someone until you had walked a mile in their moccasins—or in Thelma's case, her Manolo Blahniks. Not that she was sure exactly what she had expected from Thelma.

It just seemed odd, she thought, as she left the boat. Despite all the flowers and fruit baskets she had received, all the phone calls from celebrities, Thelma seemed very alone. Isolated, even, and ignorant of her situation. Ron's inattention to finances—he apparently had forgotten to pay the rent on the yacht and hadn't bothered to cover the check for the docking fee—had left his mother in an awkward situation. She reminded Lucy of some doomed, uncomprehending grand duchess trapped in a castle while the mob raged at the gates. It was just a matter of time before the gates fell.

On the one hand, maybe Ron had just been careless about paying his bills. Lots of people were, Lucy knew, and it didn't necessarily mean they were short of cash. On the other hand, it did seem funny that Thelma hadn't heard from any business associates or colleagues of Ron's. Wouldn't it be funny, she thought as she toiled up the hill to Main Street, if it turned out that Ron wasn't a millionaire at all? If he wasn't really the next Bill Gates? If Secure.net wasn't doing quite as well as everyone thought?

It was unlikely, she admitted to herself. Investments were strictly regulated, weren't they? Weren't there all sorts of checks and balances and rules about disclosure and insider trading and . . . Well, she admitted to herself, she wasn't exactly sure of the particulars, but it seemed impossible that everybody could be wrong about Secure.net.

The person who would know, of course, was Dorfman. She wanted to talk to him about Ron's behavior on the day he died, anyway. She paused for a moment at the corner of Main Street, checked her watch, and decided to take the car over to the Queen Vic. That way, she wouldn't have to retrace her steps to retrieve it.

She was hungry, she realized as she started the car, but there was no time to eat now. She wanted to talk to Dorfman, and then she knew she ought to stop in at Sue's and see how they were coping. *If* they were coping. Whatever they were doing over there.

It was confusing, Lucy admitted. There was Thelma, mother of the next Bill Gates, about to be evicted from her luxurious yacht, but nonetheless showered with formal expressions of sympathy from people Lucy knew only as names in print. And on the other side of town, Sue had cut herself off from the friends and neighbors who genuinely cared about her and Sidra and wanted to ease their grief with a hearty casserole, a bunch of zinnias from the garden, or just by sitting with them awhile.

One step at a time, Lucy reminded herself. First she was going to talk to Dorfman, and then she'd tackle Sue.

* * *

Lucy had only driven a short way down Main Street before she realized something was going on. Several police cars were pulled up in front of the Queen Vic, and another was blocking the driveway. She parked in a shady spot on a side street, then grabbed her camera and notebook and hurried back to the inn. When she tried to mount the steps to the porch, however, a uniformed officer turned her away.

"Why can't I go in?" demanded Lucy. "My daughter works here and"—she patted her oversized bag—"she forgot her lunch. I just want to give Elizabeth her lunch. It's already past one and she has low blood sugar, you see, and if she isn't careful about her diet . . ."

Lucy saw the officer's eyes glazing over. "Go on. Just make it snappy," he said.

Charging into the inn's reception area, Lucy spotted a chambermaid's cart at the end of the first-floor hall and made straight for it. Coming out of a room to fetch towels, Elizabeth blinked.

"Mom! What are you doing here?"

"What's going on? There are cops all over the place!"

"You're telling me. They were looking for Dorfman but he wasn't here, so they're searching his room. They had a warrant and everything. There must be a dozen cops up there. Nobody's supposed to go on the third floor—even the guests can't go back to their rooms." She looked at her mother. "How did you get in?"

"I told the officer I was bringing you your lunch."

"Thanks, Mom. I forgot it this morning."

"I don't have it—I just said that to get inside."

"You don't?"

"No."

"I'm starving. This is really hard work, you know."

"Can't you buy something?"

"I don't have any money. You make me put it all in the bank."

"You had thirty dollars for the week, plus tips."

"It's gone now."

Lucy rolled her eyes. "Here's five dollars. Get yourself a sandwich."

"Thanks, Mom."

It was only when she was leaving that she came to her senses. Elizabeth, starving? Not likely. The girl hadn't eaten a square meal in years. Nope, she'd been duped out of five dollars. Probably for cigarettes.

Kids, she muttered, stamping her foot on the sidewalk and hurrying to her car. You tell them smoking is bad and will make them sick, you carefully keep a smoke-free house, and what do they do? Sneak off and smoke in secret, as if she didn't know what was going on. As if Elizabeth's laundry didn't smell of cigarettes! Still fuming, she yanked the door open and plunked herself in the driver's seat. Next stop, Sue's house, she reminded herself as she put the key in the ignition. She had just turned it when a hand clamped over her mouth.

"Just drive. Don't look back. Got it?"

Frozen with fear, Lucy willed her head to nod up and down.

"I've got a gun, so don't try anything funny."

Lucy wasn't about to. It was all she could do to get the car in gear. Preparing to pull out in traffic, she instinctively glanced at the rearview mirror, but the carjacker caught the motion and flipped up the mirror. All Lucy got was a glimpse of a leather wrist band with metal studs.

"I'll tell you if it's clear," he growled. "Go! Now!"

Lucy cautiously pulled out of her parking spot and proceeded slowly down the street. Her heart was pounding and she was holding on to the steering wheel as if it were a life preserver. She tried frantically to think of some way to save herself. Maybe if she drove very slowly she would attract attention from the police officers who were standing on the curb, chatting with each other.

"Can't you go a little faster?"

So much for Plan A, she thought, pressing her foot on the gas pedal. Maybe she should try speeding.

"Just go the speed limit and nobody'll get hurt. Just get me to the interstate."

"What then?" asked Lucy, her voice quavering.

The question seemed to anger her kidnapper. "Just drive," he snarled, and she felt something cold and hard pressed against her neck.

Lucy took in a sharp breath. She didn't want to get killed; she didn't want to spend the rest of her life paralyzed. "I'll do whatever you say," she whispered.

"That's better."

She breathed a sigh of relief as the gun was removed from her neck.

"Remember, any funny stuff and I won't hesitate to use this."

"No funny stuff," she said, realizing with dismay that they were already out of town and it wasn't far to the entrance ramp to the turnpike. Once they were on the highway, she realized, her chances of rescue would be much slimmer. The farther they got from home, the greater her danger would be. She had to do something to save herself.

But what? she wondered, as the familiar landmarks slipped by one by one. They'd already passed the outlet mall and the farmhouse with the lawn full of homemade whirligigs and miniature windmills and lighthouses. The ramp was just ahead.

The toll, thought Lucy, feeling a little surge of hope. Maybe she could signal the toll attendant who handed out the cards.

"Go to the far right," the carjacker ordered.

Lucy did and pulled up at the automatic dispenser. Grabbing the ticket, she slammed her foot down on the accelerator as hard as she could, making the car lurch forward.

"Easy," he bellowed, and she felt the gun at the nape of her neck.

If she ever got out of this, she vowed as she lifted her foot off the gas pedal, she would kill Sidra. What had that silly girl ever seen in Davitz? Why had she ever gotten involved with a shady guy like that? She was certain of it now. He must have been involved in something crooked or he wouldn't have gotten himself killed and she wouldn't be exposed to this unpleasant person who was sitting in the backseat of her car, holding a gun to her head.

This was not the new economy; it was the oldest economy going, and Dorfman must have cottoned to it. That's why the cops were searching his room. Davitz couldn't have been working alone, she thought, her mind in a whirl. He had to have accomplices. Not Thelma, she didn't have a clue. And certainly not Sidra—Lucy wouldn't even entertain the thought. What about those two men in polo shirts she'd seen at the coffee shop? They had certainly looked suspicious. Lucy sent up a little prayer that it wasn't one of those hard-eyed, over-muscled men in her backseat, but she was pretty sure it must be.

"Pull into this rest area; go into the parking area for trucks."

Lucy's heart sank. This was it. He'd take the car, of course. But what was he going to do with her?

"Pull up behind that gravel truck."

Oh, no. Not knocked on the head, maybe killed, thrown into a gravel truck, and covered by a tarp. How long would it be before she was discovered? Not until the driver reached his destination, that was for sure.

"Now, listen very carefully and do exactly as I tell you. Look straight ahead, but put your hand back, palm up."

Lucy obeyed, ashamed of the way her hand shook. Something small and cold was placed in the palm of her hand. Poison? He was going to make her swallow poison?

"It's a quarter. Now I want you to get out of the car,

just walk away. Leave your keys and purse. Go straight to the rest area, wait ten minutes, and call somebody to come and get you."

Clutching the quarter and shaking, Lucy reached for the door handle, then paused as a tidal wave of anger rose within her. This was no carjacking; it must be some stupid prank of Toby's. What a lot of nerve this jerk had, terrifying her, making her drive over hell and beyond. She wasn't going to take it.

"What do you think you're doing?" she screamed, whirling around to face her kidnapper. "Like I have nothing better to do than . . . than . . ."

She stammered to a halt, recognizing Dorfman in the backseat.

"I should have known," she said. "You used me to get away from the cops."

"I had to," he said. "My car's still in the shop."

Lucy narrowed her eyes. "Did you really have a gun?"

Dorfman showed her a Swiss Army knife. "It wasn't even open."

Lucy looked him over. He didn't seem very threatening now, slumped down in the backseat. But he had been desperate enough to kidnap her. He must have a reason. He must be guilty, she thought.

"You killed Ron?"

"No!" He shook his head. "You don't understand. That whole Secure.net thing is a fraud. It's nothing but an old-fashioned pyramid scheme. There's no technological breakthrough. No business. Nothing but a glossy prospectus. He conned people—some pretty famous people—into investing."

Lucy shook her head. "How could he pull it off? It seems fantastic."

"Just say the word *Internet* or *dot com* and people are falling all over themselves to invest. He talked the stock up big in Internet chat rooms, dropping tips. Investors ate it up, falling all over each other to buy the stock and driving the price up. It's called 'pump and dump.'

When the time was right he'd sell and disappear, leaving the investors holding a lot of worthless stock."

Lucy remembered how reluctant Ron had been to submit to an interview with Dorfman, how his mother had pushed him. He'd been afraid that Dorfman would expose him. That was why he'd gotten so angry with him at the coffee shop. That was why he went looking for Dorfman the day he was killed. To buy him off? And if that failed, to get rid of him?

"Davitz had to stop the story, right? He confronted you, you had a fight, and he ended up dead. It was self-defense."

"I never saw him that night. He stole my laptop and some of my notes."

"Then why are you running away?"

"I did something illegal and I don't want to go to jail."

"What did you do? Steal a drink from the honor bar at the Queen Vic?"

"Worse than that. Illegal wiretapping. Breaking and entry. Theft."

"To get the story?"

He nodded.

Lucy considered. She'd do the same thing; she knew she would. "That doesn't sound so bad to me. I think you're overreacting. I mean, who's going to press charges? Davitz is dead, and now that the cops have your stuff, they'll figure out what he was up to. I bet if you offer to cooperate they'll work out a deal for you— probably forget the whole thing."

Dorfman looked doubtful. "You think I should go back?"

"What are your alternatives? Think about it. Are you going to leave the country? You've got some little hideout all set up in some banana republic that doesn't have an extradition treaty?"

"I wish."

"Well, then, you might as well go back and face the music."

Dorfman nodded.

"Want to sit in the front seat?" she asked, starting the car. As she waited for him to settle himself beside her, she noticed the colorful sign on the rest area building. "Listen, before we go, do you want to get a burger or something? I'm awfully hungry."

"I could use something, too," he admitted.

"Being carjacked really gives you an appetite," said Lucy, as they walked toward the fast food restaurant.

Dorfman laughed. "You did seem pretty scared."

"Let's not go there," suggested Lucy. "I could still press charges you know."

"I'll buy," offered Dorfman.

"Under the circumstances, it's the least you could do."

Chapter Nineteen

Lucy didn't take any chances when they got back to Tinker's Cove. She drove straight to the police station and watched to make sure Dorfman went inside.

Then, alone in the car, she paused to consider her next step. She knew she ought to go straight to Sue's, but she hesitated. Things had changed. Now, Sidra had to face the fact that the man she loved was not only dead, but he wasn't the man she thought he was. Of all his deceits, Lucy thought Ron's dishonesty to Sidra the worst of all. Inevitably, she would have to wonder if he had ever loved her at all, or if she was just part of a larger plan. A conduit to Norah Hemmings, perhaps, and her fortune.

The thought made Lucy shudder. Could Sidra have been part of the scheme? Before the shower, Lucy wouldn't have entertained the thought for even a second. But after seeing the company she was keeping these days, and the way she behaved over Molly's potholders, she had to wonder. No, she decided, Sidra's bad behavior at the shower was just that and nothing more. Her head may have been temporarily turned, but at heart Sidra didn't have a dishonest bone in her body. Lucy had seen her grow up; she had watched her mature into an independent young woman she thought of as a role model for her own daughters. She knew her as well as she knew anyone.

But how could you be sure you knew someone, Lucy wondered. Take Bill, for example. He was honest as the day was long; he wore his heart on his sleeve. He could never play poker. Heck, thought Lucy with a smile, he couldn't even beat the kids at Old Maid. They soon learned to read his expressions when picking cards from his hand, and he always got stuck with the queen.

But even Bill had secrets. Lucy had been shocked to find a speeding ticket he'd never mentioned to her when she cleaned out his truck a few months ago, and she'd often wondered if he'd simply forgotten or if he had intentionally hidden it from her. Of course, a speeding ticket was hardly comparable to defrauding investors of millions of dollars. Nevertheless, she remembered how hurt and angry she'd felt when she found it, and she could well imagine how betrayed Sidra would feel when the news came out. She would be devastated. How could she ever trust her feelings again after being duped so cruelly. But even worse, Lucy realized with a shock, would have been her fate if she had married Ron. What sort of life would she have had then, smeared and tarnished by association with a swindler? No, thought Lucy, sadly shaking her head. Awful as her situation was, Sidra had had a very lucky escape. And that was what she would tell her.

Lucy was just a few blocks from Sue's house when she realized that she might have stumbled on a motive for Sue, or Sid, to kill Ron. Maybe they had discovered Ron was a swindler and had killed him to save Sidra from marrying him. Or maybe they'd just confronted him with the truth, and things had gotten out of hand. Lucy could just see it: an angry Sid, a defiant Ron. If Ron had pushed Sid, he might well have shoved him back, causing him to fall off the dock. He could easily have hit his head on a boat, or on the dock itself.

Lucy braked in front of Sue's house, but she was strongly tempted to drive away. Suddenly, she wanted to forget the whole thing. Sweep it under the rug. Make it go away. She didn't want to face the possibility that Sue was involved in Ron's murder.

Of course, she realized, if Ron's dishonesty was news to the Finches, if it turned out that they thought he was a genuine millionaire, then they wouldn't have had a motive to kill him. Not exactly, she admitted to herself. They would have had a motive: the fact that they didn't like him and didn't want Sidra to marry him. But in light of her new knowledge about Ron, there were probably a lot of other people who had more compelling reasons to kill him. Investors, for example, who had trusted him with their money. Journalists who had written glowing articles about him. Celebrities and society glitterati who had welcomed him with open arms. No, she thought, climbing out of the car. The circle of suspects had widened quite a lot.

Straightening her shoulders, she walked up to the front door and rang the bell, hoping her courage wouldn't desert her. As it was, when one of the bridesmaids opened the door, she almost turned tail and ran.

"I'm a friend of Sue's," she began, trying to explain herself to the sleek creature with almond eyes who was acting as doorkeeper. "I remember you from the shower. You're . . . Kat!"

"No. I'm Susanna. Come on in."

Lucy followed her into the living room, where Sidra was seated on the couch between the other two bridesmaids, Kat and Lily. The darkened room was filled with dozens of flower arrangements and the air was heavy with their scent. Lucy went to her, bending down and taking her hands.

"Hi, sweetheart. How are you doing?"

"I'm still kind of stunned, I think," she said.

Have I got a surprise for you, thought Lucy, as the bridesmaids clucked sympathetically. Today they were again dressed almost identically, in sleeveless black knit shirts and khaki Capri pants. How did they do it? Lucy wondered. Did they discuss what to wear at breakfast, or was there some unwritten code for suitable dress appropriate to any occasion?

"I know everything's changed," continued Sidra, "but it hasn't really sunk in yet. I mean, I keep thinking of things I have to do for the wedding, and then I remember there isn't going to be a wedding."

The bridesmaids sighed in unison.

"No wedding," repeated Susanna in a sad voice.

For a minute, Lucy wondered if the grief that was so palpable in the room was actually for Ron, or for the wedding. Then, remembering her original mission, she asked if Sue was home.

"She's on the back porch," said Susanna, apparently the official hostess. "Can I show you the way?"

"I know it, thanks," said Lucy. Again, she grasped Sidra's hand. "I know you don't believe this now, but things have a way of working out."

"Thanks, Aunt Lucy."

Lucy smiled politely at the bridesmaids and continued through the dining room and kitchen out to the back porch that overlooked the garden. Sue was indeed there, lying on a chaise with her eyes closed. When Lucy opened the door, Sue's eyes flew open and she sat up.

"I didn't mean to startle you," Lucy said.

"Oh, it's only you."

Lucy thought she seemed awfully relieved. "Who were you expecting?"

"The worst," Sue said darkly.

"Any word from Sid?" Lucy asked, keeping her voice casual.

"I told you, he went fishing. I may not hear from him for a week or more."

"There's no way to contact him?" Lucy persisted.

"No," snapped Sue. "I don't know why you're making so much out of this."

"Come on," said Lucy, losing patience. "Admit it. You have been acting kind of oddly."

"Well, my daughter's fiancé has died suddenly, I have a heartbroken daughter on my hands, and my house is filled with bridesmaids in mourning. I don't know . . . how do you think I should act?" Sue's eyes flashed angrily. "And I don't need you to keep bugging me."

"Whoa," said Lucy, taking a seat next to her friend. "Let's start over. I have some interesting information about Ron."

"Like what? He's not a millionaire, he's a billionaire?"

"He's broke. The whole thing was a swindle."

Sue's chin dropped. "What?"

"It was all a big hoax. He hasn't paid his rent on the yacht; he owes money for docking fees. It's all over town. Plus, I talked to that writer from New York, Dorfman, and he has proof it was all a scam. A swindle. A big fraud. He's talking to the police right now."

Sue, who had been hanging on every word, collapsed back on the chaise and began to laugh. "That's great," she said. "That's fabulous."

This wasn't quite the reaction Lucy had expected. "Why?"

"Because now I don't have to pretend I'm sorry that the little weasel is dead. I don't have to go through the motions of receiving callers; I don't have to fill my house with gladiolus; I don't have to eat Franny Small's Austrian ravioli. It's all over. I'm going to tell Sidra."

"Do you think that's a good idea . . ." began Lucy, but Sue was already on her feet. She dashed into the living room and opened the blinds, letting the sun in and startling Sidra and the others.

"Do you know what Lucy found out?" she began, standing in front of Sidra and placing her hands on her hips. "Ron was a crook. He wasn't a millionaire after all. There's no money; there's nothing at all. He was a big phony."

"That can't be true . . ." began Sidra.

The bridesmaids glanced uneasily at each other.

"It is!" Sue proclaimed triumphantly. "Ask Lucy."

Four sets of eyes fastened on Lucy.

She shrugged apologetically and nodded.

Sidra began sobbing hysterically. Lily passed her a box of tissues, then stood up and reached for her purse.

"We can see you're upset," she said, patting Sidra on the head.

"I think we'd better go," said Lily, sliding smoothly along the couch, away from Sidra. Reaching the end, she stood up.

"You've got my cell phone number if you need anything," said Kat, picking up her excruciatingly fashionable mini-tote bag.

Together, the three slipped out the front door. From the window, Lucy could see them pausing on the front walk for a quick gabfest, full of exclamations and gestures. Then they hurried down the walk, got in Norah's big SUV, and drove away.

"Good riddance to bad rubbish," said Sue, sitting beside Sidra.

"Why did they leave?" demanded Sidra, dabbing at her eyes.

"Because you're not going to be marrying a millionaire, that's why. Because you're not going to be their ticket to café society."

Sidra glared at her. "How can you say that? They're my friends."

"Well, where are they, then?" Sue asked, gesturing with an open palm. "They heard he was broke, and they vamoosed. Actions speak louder than words, honey."

Sidra looked at her mother, then at Lucy.

"I can't believe I've been so stupid," she whispered. "Do you think he ever intended to really marry me?"

"Count yourself lucky," said Lucy. "You had a close call."

Sidra sat utterly still and white-faced for the longest

time. Then, suddenly, she staggered to her feet, blinking like someone coming out of a long sleep.

"God, I hate gladiolus!" she exclaimed. "Is there something we can do with these flowers?"

"Toss 'em out," suggested Sue, picking up an arrangement.

"No," said Sidra, "that would be a waste. Let's take them over to the nursing home."

"You're back!" Sue exclaimed happily, beaming at her daughter. "It's the real Sidra."

"I'm sorry, Mom," she said, giving Sue a hug. "I've been a real jerk."

"You're forgiven." Sue smiled at Lucy. "Come on! Let's get these flowers into the car."

Chapter Twenty

Checking her watch, Lucy realized she had better get a move on or she would be late picking up the kids. She gave Sue and Sidra a wave and headed straight for the Queen Vic, and this time there were no police cars obstructing the driveway. She drove right up to the porch, where Elizabeth was sitting in a rocking chair waiting for her.

"Wow, Mom, you're actually on time," observed Elizabeth.

"Miracles happen," Lucy said serenely.

And it was true, she thought. That was how she felt. For once, order had been restored to her world and things seemed to be working out right. The news that Ron had been a swindler had somehow come as a great relief. Not only to Sue and Sidra, Lucy realized, but to the whole town. Now Ron's death wasn't a Tinker's Cove affair; it wasn't linked to the wedding. It was much more likely, thought Lucy, that Ron's death was a result of his illegal activities. Now the investigation would extend far beyond Tinker's Cove.

In fact, she noticed as she pulled into her usual spot at the harbor, the white TV satellite trucks had almost all gone. Only the Portland station's truck remained.

Lucy honked her horn. From the Lady L, bobbing at its usual mooring in the harbor, she saw Toby wave. A few minutes later he was in the dinghy, rowing to shore.

As they waited, Lucy was surprised to see crew members on the Sea Witch cast off the lines and weigh anchor. The engines hummed, and the huge yacht slowly pulled away from the dock. Was Thelma aboard, Lucy wondered, or had she been jettisoned? For a moment, she had a crazy vision of Thelma, in jewels and high heels, attempting to hitch a ride on the interstate. She giggled.

"What's so funny?" Elizabeth asked.

Feeling guilty, Lucy erased the thought from her mind.

"Nothing," she said, spying Thelma's tiny figure on the upper deck.

She couldn't help feeling a surge of sympathy for the woman. Her society friends would certainly abandon her as soon as the news about Ron got out, just like Sidra's bridesmaids had deserted her. She would not only have to deal with her grief for Ron, but she would also have to construct a new life for herself.

Toby pulled the car door open and plunked down in the backseat.

"You're awfully quiet," said Lucy, putting the car in gear and driving off. "Is something the matter?"

"I'm scared, Mom," said Toby. "When we got back in this afternoon, some cops were waiting for Geoff. He figured they just wanted to ask him a few questions, but they took him away with them."

"They arrested Geoff?" Elizabeth's voice was shrill.

"I guess so. They made him go with them."

Lucy didn't like the sound of this. It seemed as if Geoff was now a suspect in Ron's murder. She felt a tight little knot of anxiety forming in her stomach.

"Mom, you've got to do something about this," demanded Elizabeth, eager to defend her idol. "Geoff would never do anything bad."

"They searched the boat, too," Toby added. "After they took him away. I didn't know what to do. They had a warrant and everything, so I didn't try to stop them."

"They have a right to search," said Lucy. "Did they find anything?"

"They took stuff away, but I don't know what it was."

"I thought this was a democracy," Elizabeth muttered.

"What could he possibly have on the boat?" asked Lucy, wondering if this sudden police interest in Geoff was a result of their conversation with Dorfman. Once they eliminated him, Geoff would probably be next on their list. It was no secret that Geoff and Sidra had been dating before she took up with Ron. As a jilted boyfriend, he would be a prime suspect.

"Just research data about lobsters—why would they want that?"

"They probably don't know what it is," Lucy suggested, reaching out to pat Elizabeth's thigh. "Once they figure it out, they'll have to let him go."

"Are you sure, Mom?" asked Elizabeth.

"I'm sure," said Lucy, wishing she were half as convinced as she sounded. She turned into the drive at the Animal Friends Day Camp to pick up Zoe and Sara.

Next morning, a radio news report confirmed that Geoff Rumford was assisting police in their investigation but was not considered a suspect. He had been questioned and released.

"Does that mean he's off the hook?" Elizabeth asked as she nibbled on an English muffin. It was her day off, but she was up early. Lance was taking her out for the day.

"Not necessarily," admitted Lucy. "They can't charge him without evidence. They could be putting together a case against him."

"But he's innocent!" declared Elizabeth.

"Well, you and I think so, but the police may have a

different idea." Lucy sent up a private little prayer. "It will all work out in the end."

"It better, or I'll be out of a job," Toby added, slathering great quantities of cream cheese on a bagel. "I could probably get something else," he continued, "but the project is showing real promise. Geoff said so the other day. It would be a shame if he had to stop now that he's so close. You know how many people around here depend on lobsters."

"That's for sure," Lucy agreed.

"Mom, isn't there something you can do?" asked Elizabeth. "You know a lot of cops, like Barney and that lieutenant. You could tell them they're wrong, couldn't you?"

Lucy gave Elizabeth a rueful smile. "I don't think Lieutenant Horowitz would appreciate my advice."

"C'mon, Mom," added Toby. "Geoff's a good guy. I like working for him."

Lucy looked from one earnest young face to the other. How could she refuse? Especially since she might have important information. What about those suspicious men in polo shirts? Had the police questioned them? Did they even know about them? It wouldn't hurt to pay a visit to Barney and ask him to pass the word along.

"Okay," she said, watching as they both broke into huge smiles. "But don't get all excited. It probably won't make any difference."

An hour later, Lucy was making her usual stop at the harbor, dropping Toby off. Geoff was already on the boat, which had returned to its usual slip, bent over the bait boxes. He waved cheerfully as Toby walked down the dock, past the police officer who was posted there.

It was a tactic the local police had adopted recently, and Lucy didn't approve of it. When they suspected someone but didn't have enough evidence to press charges, they would keep the "subject" under observation. The official explanation was that surveillance was necessary in case the subject attempted to flee, but Lucy didn't buy it. She thought it was simply a tactic to apply pressure to someone who was under suspicion in hopes that he or she would crack. Adding to the pressure was the presence of the Portland video crew.

A boat engine roared into life, and Lucy turned to see who it was. To her surprise, it was a blue-and-white police boat. They were apparently intending to follow the Lady L as Geoff and Toby went about their day's work at sea.

The very idea disgusted her. She wanted to protest to someone about this injustice. Spotting Chuck Swift gassing up his boat at the fuel pump, she hurried over to him.

"Look at that!" she said, pointing out the police boat. "Do you see what they're doing? It looks like they're going to follow the Lady L."

Chuck replaced the cap on his fuel tank and jumped onto the dock beside her.

"What's it all about?" he asked.

"They think Geoff killed Davitz."

"That's a crime?" he asked with a perfectly straight face. "Next thing you know, it'll be illegal to step on a spider or trap a rat."

"Shame on you," chided Lucy. "For all his faults, he was a human being. He didn't deserve to be murdered."

"I'm still not convinced it was murder," said Chuck. "He could have slipped and hit his head falling in the water. It's happened before."

"Really?" Lucy was skeptical.

"Yeah." Chuck nodded. "That's how Carrie's grandfather died. Slipped on a piece of bait and fell overboard, hitting his head on a bollard. They pulled him right out, but he was already dead." Chuck looked toward the open water. "Fishing is real dangerous. More dangerous than people realize. You're moving heavy stuff around on a slippery deck that like as not is rolling with the waves; you can get crushed. You can fall overboard—you know, most fishermen can't swim. They're superstitious about it. Then there's the machinery. You can lose your fingers in a winch, get burned trying to fix a stalled engine. You want to know the truth, it's a terrible way of making a living," he said cheerfully. Then his face grew serious. "Carrie wants me to stop, because of the baby."

"Are you going to?"

He gave his head a quick shake. "Nope."

Lucy understood that fishing was in his blood; he could never give it up. "Were you down here on the Fourth?" she asked.

"Sure. Took the whole clan out in the boat to see the fireworks."

"I mean earlier. In the afternoon. Around the time Ron got killed."

He cocked his head. "You're not playing detective, are you?"

"No. Nothing like that. I just wondered if you might have seen something unusual."

"Well, it was a holiday," he said, clamping his hands on his suspenders. "It wasn't a regular working day. There were a lot of pleasure boaters, tourists. It was real busy down here."

Hearing a shout, they turned and saw the harbormaster hurrying down the dock toward them.

"Why don't you ask him?" suggested Chuck, reaching down and untying his boat.

"Hey, you! What do you think you're doing?" Wiggins's face was red and his whiskers were quivering with outrage.

"I'm going about my business," said Chuck, pulling himself to his full height and facing Wiggins. "Have you got a problem with that?"

Testosterone, thought Lucy. Great stuff. Made men behave like roosters.

"I've got a problem with you, Swift." Wiggins pointed a nicotine-stained finger at Chuck. "Can't you read?"

"I can read," Chuck said slowly. "But I'm not sure about you."

"Well, if you can read, how come you can't read that sign?"

Lucy followed Wiggins's finger and saw a brand-new sign limiting fueling time to fifteen minutes.

"You can't be serious," scoffed Chuck.

"It's town policy, and it's my job to enforce it."

"That's the problem with you, Wiggins," said Chuck, leaning back on his heels and narrowing his eyes. "You can't think for yourself. This is just one example. Okay. There's a fifteen-minute time limit. I'll go along with that. Good idea, when there's a lot of boats that need fuel. But right now, do you see anybody else waiting to use the pump?" He waved a hand at the nearly empty harbor. "Not a soul. So what's the big deal?"

"The big deal is that you think you can do whatever you want. Well, listen to me," said Wiggins, thrusting his whiskered face in Chuck's and giving him a little shove. "I'm the boss around here."

Chuck staggered backward, then regained his balance and nimbly jumped into his boat. He grabbed the gaff and turned to face Wiggins.

"You want to get rough?" he asked, challenging him.

"Listen, fellas," said Lucy, stepping in front of Wiggins. "Maybe you both ought to cool down a little. I don't want to have to testify against either one of you."

Chuck laughed, tossed his gaff aside and started the engine. Giving a wave, he pulled away from the dock.

"Hey!" yelled Wiggins. "It's pump and pay. That's the policy. No credit!" Realizing Chuck was already out of earshot, he turned on Lucy. "And what are you doing here?" he demanded. "Did you get authorization?"

"No, I'm not authorized," said Lucy, through her teeth. "But I wouldn't worry about that if I were you, since if it wasn't for me, you'd be treading water right now."

Turning on her heel, Lucy marched back to the car. It wasn't until she was out of the parking lot and on Main Street that she realized she'd missed her chance to ask Wiggins if he'd seen any suspicious characters on the wharf around the time that Davitz was killed.

Resolving to try to talk with him that evening when she picked up Toby, she headed over to the police station. With luck, she could catch Barney leaving for his usual morning coffee break.

When she arrived, however, the usually empty lobby was full of people, as if a meeting had just ended. In the middle of them all was Lieutenant Horowitz. Lucy quickly turned away in hopes of avoiding him, but she wasn't quick enough.

"My favorite reporter," he said, without much enthusiasm.

"Looks like you've got quite a crowd here," said Lucy, pulling out her notebook. "What's going on?"

Horowitz shrugged. "Just bringing everybody up to speed on the investigation," he said.

Lucy glanced at the mix of plainclothes and uniformed officers that were crowding the lobby. "Are all these officers involved in investigating Davitz's murder?" she asked.

Horowitz worked his long upper lip. "We take murder very seriously," he said.

"Not this seriously," protested Lucy. "I've never seen more than a handful of officers assigned to one case. Are you sure Davitz's murder isn't tied into some larger investigation?"

Horowitz's gray eyes were blank. "I can't comment on that at this time," he said.

"Well, when do you think you will be able to comment?"

"I'm not a fortune teller, Mrs. Stone. I can't predict the future."

Frustrated, Lucy let out a long sigh.

"I really, really think you're on the wrong track," said Lucy. "Geoff Rumford is not the murderer." She paused. "Did you know two thugs in polo shirts were seen following Davitz shortly before his death?"

Horowitz's eyes widened with surprise. "Really?"

"Yes, really," said Lucy, a note of triumph in her voice. "What do you say to that?"

"As I said earlier, I really can't comment." He turned to go, then stopped. A smile tickled his mouth. "Agents Heller and Morton will be interested to hear you mistook them for thugs," he said, chuckling.

"Agents? You mean those guys are feds? Were they investigating Davitz *before* he got killed?"

"Like I said earlier, Mrs. Stone, I really can't comment."

Tossing her head back and rolling her eyes, Lucy stormed out the door. On the steps, she ran smack into Officer Barney Culpepper's huge barrel chest.

"Take it easy, Lucy," he said. "Are you all right?"

"Sorry, Barney. It's just that Lieutenant Horowitz is so maddening. I swear, if I had a penny for every time that man told me he couldn't comment, I'd be a rich woman."

Barney chuckled.

"I don't think it's funny at all," Lucy fumed. "I just don't get the humor."

At this, Barney's belly began to heave with laughter. "It's just . . . it's just . . . if you could see yourself," he said.

Lucy looked at him suspiciously. "Is my hair sticking up or something? Have I got spinach between my teeth?"

He shook his head helplessly.

"What? What's so funny?"

He leaned against the railing and took a deep breath, then another.

"It was just the expression on your face," he said, gaining control of himself. "You looked so mad."

"I am mad. I went in with perfectly good intentions of sharing information, and Horowitz made fun of me."

"What information?" Barney wiped his face with an enormous handkerchief.

"I just wanted to make sure he knew about those guys who were following Davitz."

"Heller and Morton. They're FBI."

"Well, thanks for sharing."

"Look, I gotta take care of myself, you know? I'm getting close to retiring, and I don't want to blow it. Know what I mean?"

Lucy felt chagrined. "I know. I'm sorry, Barney. I'm just upset that suspicion seems to be focusing on Geoff Rumford, that's all."

The door opened and several officers exited the building. Barney took Lucy's elbow and pulled her to the side of the stone steps.

"You just never know," he said. "I've been surprised plenty of times before. The nicest people seem to do the worst things. Like that youth minister last year? Remember him?" He rolled his eyes.

Lucy remembered. He'd been charged with twenty-three counts of corrupting a minor.

"Geoff's not like that," insisted Lucy. "And he's not a murderer, either. That research project could do a lot for this town, you know. Toby's working for him this summer, and he says they're making progress."

"Toby's working for him?"

The note of concern in Barney's voice alarmed her. "Is that a problem?" she asked.

"Well," he drawled, hitching up his heavy utility belt and lowering his voice. "This is just between you and me, and it's not for publication, get my gist?"

Lucy swallowed hard. "I get it."

"Maybe Toby should start lookin' for another job."
He cocked an eyebrow and gave her a glance loaded
with meaning. "That's what I'd do, if I were him."

For a second, Lucy felt as if she'd suddenly lost her
footing and she grabbed Barney's arm.

She shook her head. "I don't believe it. It wasn't
Geoff; I just know it. They've got the wrong guy."

Barney patted her hand with a huge paw. "Lucy,
they've got a witness. An eyewitness."

"Big deal," said Lucy, rallying to Geoff's defense.
"They've done studies, you know, and it turns out that
eyewitnesses are not very reliable. They're wrong most
of the time, like that poor guy on death row. Eyewitnesses absolutely said he was the man, but when they
did DNA testing it turned out it couldn't have been
him. They had to let him go."

"Well, then, my advice to Geoff would be to get some
of that DNA," said Barney.

"Somehow you're not making me feel better," said
Lucy, before turning and walking slowly toward her car.

Chapter Twenty-one

Back in the Subaru, Lucy faced the inevitable. She couldn't put it off any longer; she had to go back to the harbor and talk to Wiggins. The harbor was where Davitz was killed, she reasoned, so that's where she would most likely find a lead to this so-called eyewitness. As harbormaster, Wiggins was almost always there, and he would certainly know to whom the police had been talking in the past few days. In fact, Lucy wondered if Wiggins himself might be the witness. There was certainly no love lost between him and Geoff, and he would probably be more than happy to get Geoff in trouble. Of course, getting him to cooperate wouldn't be easy. Maybe if she held out the promise of some favorable coverage in the *Pennysaver*? It would certainly be questionable from an ethical standpoint, she admitted to herself, but it might work. Heck, it was worth a try.

She parked and trotted up to the harbormaster's office, noticing as she approached that it looked deserted. The office was about the size of a tollbooth and had windows on all four sides, making it easy to tell if anyone was there. She pulled on the door, thinking she might find a note with Wiggins's whereabouts, or a phone number, but it was locked.

Momentarily stumped, she scanned the harbor. There was no sign of the Lady L or the police boat, but a number of small sailboats were tacking back and forth near the yacht club on the point. Probably sailing lessons.

On this side of the bay, there wasn't much activity. The boats bobbing at their moorings or settled in their berths seemed deserted. The brand-new sign by the gas pump caught her eye, and she remembered how close Wiggins and Chuck Swift had come to a fight earlier that morning. She remembered Wiggins's attempt to jab Chuck, and how Chuck responded by reaching for his gaff.

Her stomach tightened and she suddenly felt very cold. Could that be how it happened? Had Davitz challenged Chuck, or made some sort of wisecrack about local yokels? And had Chuck reached for his gaff and knocked Davitz on the head? Knowing how hot-tempered Chuck could be, Lucy thought it all too likely.

Considering how similar Chuck and Geoff looked, in identical yellow fishing pants and with heads of sandy-colored hair, it would have been easy enough for an eyewitness to mistake one for the other. They were both young and lean, both about six feet tall. From any distance, it would be impossible to tell one from the other.

Lost in thought, Lucy was surprised when Lance Hemmings and Elizabeth pulled up to the dock in a beautifully refinished vintage cigarette boat. The craft had a gleaming mahogany hull and sleek lines. Despite her bulk, she was built for speed, and the enormous 1200-horsepower inboard engine could certainly supply it.

"Nice boat," she said. "A present from your mom?"

Lance, like Elizabeth, had just graduated from high school. Norah had told her he was planning to go to Brown University in the fall.

"How'd you know?" he asked, blushing.

Lucy thought he was awfully good-looking, now that

he had given up the orange hair and had removed the ring he used to wear in his nose. He'd filled out nicely, too. Formerly a beanpole, he'd bulked up and was now nicely muscled.

"Lucky guess," she said, smiling. "I don't suppose you think you're taking my daughter out in that thing?"

"Mom!" protested Elizabeth.

"Just for a picnic out on Metinnicut Island," he said. "It's not far and I won't go fast, I promise."

Lucy looked doubtful. "Not go fast? I don't believe it. Maybe I'd better come along and chaperon."

Lucy was only teasing; she had no intention of tagging along with Elizabeth and Lance. Elizabeth, true to form, rose to the bait.

"Mom! Are you crazy? You can't come with us!"

"Why not, Elizabeth? I'm good company, aren't I, Lance?"

Lance was a very well brought-up boy. "Of course you are, Mrs. Stone." He squared his shoulders. "We'd be glad to have you."

Lucy laughed. "No. You two go on and have a good time."

Elizabeth looked very relieved.

"Are you sure?" asked Lance.

"I'm really sure," said Lucy. "I was only joking. You go on and have a good time. Just don't forget to keep your life jackets on."

"Sure thing." Lance paused. "I could take you for a little spin around the harbor."

Lucy looked at the boat. It was gorgeous.

"Just a short one," she said.

In a moment, Lance was standing on the dock beside her, offering his arm so she could lower herself into the boat. Taking a seat, Lucy admired the boat's luxurious fittings while Elizabeth reached into the locker for the life jackets. She was zipping hers up when she heard sirens and looked up to see a line of police cruisers rolling into the parking lot with lights flashing.

That was no information meeting at the police sta-
tion, she realized. It had been a briefing. No wonder
Barney had told her Toby should think about a new job.
He'd known they were planning to arrest Geoff any
minute; the patrol boat was probably escorting the Lady
L back to the harbor at this very moment.

Lucy looked toward the mouth of the cove, scanning
the horizon for the Lady L. It was lucky she was here, she
thought. Toby would be upset—maybe frightened, and
certainly angry. Hopefully she could prevent him from
doing something he'd regret later.

Lost in thought, she was taken completely by surprise when the boat lurched suddenly. Grabbing the
taffrail that ran along the side of the boat, she turned
just in time to see Wiggins knock Lance off his feet,
onto the dock. Next thing she knew, he had taken the
wheel and the boat lurched forward; she and Elizabeth
were thrown violently back against the cushioned seat.
Lucy grasped Elizabeth's hand with one hand, and held
on tightly to the rail with the other. Back on the dock,
she saw a cluster of officers standing together, looking
across the growing expanse of water at the boat. The
group, Lucy realized with dismay as they sped across the
cove, was steadily shrinking and would soon be little
more than a dark-blue dot on the horizon.

When they passed Quisset Point, they were traveling
at such high speed that the bow of the boat was in
midair. Elizabeth had broken free from her grasp and
was attempting to climb up the deck to reach Wiggins.
Lucy yelled at her to sit down, but she couldn't hear her
own voice over the roar of the engine. Grabbing the
taffrail, she managed to pull herself to her feet and
tumbled against Elizabeth, bringing her back into the
seat with her.

Elizabeth yelled something at her, but she couldn't
make it out. She signaled to Elizabeth that they should
stay put, and Elizabeth nodded agreement. Just staying
in the seat was becoming increasingly difficult; if they

attempted to stand up, they would risk being tossed overboard. They each found handholds and hung on for dear life.

Focusing her attention on Wiggins, Lucy realized he wasn't paying as much attention to the boat as she would like. He kept glancing at her and Elizabeth, kept checking the horizon behind them, and only occasionally glanced ahead. That was inviting disaster in this rocky water. Lucy was terrified he would smash into a submerged boulder, killing them all.

She looked back, hoping to see rescuers pursuing them, but the only boat in sight was a small speck in the distance. Her heart sank when it disappeared from view. Tears stung her eyes and she tried to tell herself it was because of the wind whipping at her face, but she knew she was truly terrified. Out in the open water it was cool, too, and she was shivering. Elizabeth's teeth were chattering, and she was crying, too.

When the boat hit an obstacle—thankfully something not too large—and went soaring into the air only to land with a smack, Lucy realized she had to act. Wiggins was out of his head and didn't care if he—or they—lived or died.

Desperate, she looked about the boat for some sort of weapon. All she could find was a net on a long pole, neatly stowed in clamps along the side board. She tapped Elizabeth on the arm and pointed to it. Elizabeth waited until Wiggins was looking the other way and grabbed for it. It clattered to the deck, but the noise was covered by the engines.

Lucy dropped to her knees and, bracing her feet against the side, managed to get close enough to grab the net. Her hands, she realized, were trembling, and her breath was coming in short gasps. *Easy,* she told herself, and she took a single deep breath. Then, using every bit of strength she possessed, she rose to her knees, inch by painful inch, and hurled the net over Wiggins's head. Elizabeth dove for the loose pole and grabbed hold of it, hanging on fiercely as Wiggins struggled to free himself. The pole jerked wildly and Elizabeth was in danger of losing it until Lucy also grabbed hold. Together they were able to jerk Wiggins off his feet; Elizabeth could only keep him pinned to the deck for a second, but it was long enough for Lucy to pull the key out of the ignition and toss it overboard.

Jumping to his feet as the boat slowed, he screamed at them, "What did you do that for?" His face was red as a boiled lobster; the tendons on his neck stood out and his eyes were bulging. He'd lost his cap and his wispy hair was standing on end; his whiskers were quivering.

Sensing his raw rage, Lucy wondered if she'd made a big mistake. Now she and Elizabeth were marooned, alone in the middle of the empty sea with a madman.

"Take it easy," she said, in the tone she used when Kudo spied the neighbor's cat crossing the yard.

It usually worked on Kudo. Wiggins, however, reached for the net and snapped the pole in half. Taking the end, he began dancing around and threatening Lucy and Elizabeth with the sharp end.

"Stop it!" she yelled, in the tone of voice she used when Kudo ran off with Toby's expensive new sneakers. "Give me that."

Her eyes locked on Wiggins. His, she saw, were a weak, watery blue. She was determined to stare him down. After what seemed an eternity, he blinked.

"Give me the stick," she said, speaking slowly and deliberately.

He dropped it and kicked it across the deck to her.

"Thank you. Now, do you want to tell me what this is all about?"

For a moment, Wiggins seemed puzzled. He looked around himself, as if seeing the boat and the water for the first time.

"They were coming to get me."

"Who?" asked Lucy gently. "Who was coming to get you?"

She wouldn't have been surprised if he'd said men in white coats or creepy, slimy bugs or gigantic dinosaurs. What he did say surprised her.

"The cops."

"The cops? Why would they come for you? They were coming for Geoff Rumford."

Elizabeth gasped.

"I told 'em I saw him do it," he said, "but I didn't think they believed me."

"They believed you all right," Lucy told him. Under her breath she added, "until you ran."

"I knew Geoff didn't do it." Elizabeth was triumphant. "*You* did it!"

Lucy silenced her with a glance.

Wiggins let out a long sigh and leaned against the side of the boat. He had grown pale and Lucy thought he looked exhausted. He shrugged.

"He was in my face, yelling at me. Telling me the parade float was all my fault, that nobody respected me. That I didn't have things under control at the harbor." He paused. "He said I was an idiot."

"That must have made you angry," Lucy suggested gently.

"You bet it made me mad. Who was he to tell me how to do my job? I bent over backward for that guy, all so the town could make some money and fix up the harbor. I didn't have to do it, you know. I could have told him to take it as it was or leave, but I didn't. I tried to do everything he wanted."

"You took a lot of criticism for it, too."

"I did." Wiggins nodded. "But he was just going on and on at me. He just wouldn't shut up. It was like this noise coming from his mouth, but no words. Just noise, ringing in my ears. And his mouth kept moving and moving, it wouldn't stop. So I pulled my gun out of my holster, but even that didn't shut him up. I finally hit him on the head."

"What happened then?"

"He stopped talking and then he fell down. I figured I'd knocked him out. That was all I meant to do, I swear. I didn't mean to kill him. I waited for him to stir, but nothing happened. He was real still. I reached for his arm—to take his pulse—but couldn't find it. That's when I realized he was dead, and I'd killed him." He looked up at her, tears brimming in his eyes. "I couldn't face it. How could I tell the commission?"

Lucy had a fleeting thought that the commission would probably vote to approve the harbormaster's action.

"So you rolled him into the water?"

His head gave a little jerk.

He was pitiful, thought Lucy. You couldn't help but feel sorry for him.

"Look!" exclaimed Elizabeth. "It's the Lady L."

From across the water, the Lady L and its police escort were proceeding steadily toward them. Drawing alongside, Geoff leaped into the speedboat.

"Is everybody all right?"

"We're fine," said Lucy as a couple of police officers clambered aboard and cuffed Wiggins.

"I'm a little shaky," whispered Elizabeth.

Geoff pulled his sweatshirt off and gently slipped it over Elizabeth's head. When her face emerged, she smiled weakly at him. Wrapping an arm around her waist, he helped her climb aboard the Lady L. Then he turned and gave Lucy a hand up.

While Geoff fussed over Elizabeth, pouring her a hot cup of coffee, Toby followed the officer's instructions and fastened a line to the speedboat so they could tow it in.

"We heard the police call on the radio and started looking for you as soon as we heard," Geoff told them. "Do you have any idea where you are?"

"Not at all," whispered Elizabeth, batting her eyelashes at Geoff.

"Snowden's Bank."

"That far?" Lucy was shocked.

Geoff nodded, watching as the police transferred the handcuffed harbormaster to the patrol boat.

Wiggins didn't resist, but once aboard, he cast a mournful parting glance at the cigarette boat.

"That's one beaut of a boat," he said and spit over the side.

Chapter Twenty-two

Geoff didn't waste any time getting back to Tinker's Cove. He ran the Lady L's engine at full throttle, but the patrol boat was much faster and was already at the dock when they arrived. Word of Wiggins's desperate flight and arrest had spread quickly, and a crowd of curious onlookers had gathered in the parking lot. Still shivering and huddled in a blanket, Lucy observed the scene from the Lady L as Geoff maneuvered the lobster boat into her old berth.

Eventually, Wiggins was taken from the patrol boat and transferred, in handcuffs, to a cruiser, under the watchful eyes of the crowd and the TV cameras. He was gone when the group aboard the Lady L finally disembarked and began making their way along the floating walkway. As soon as Geoff set foot on the solid wood of the pier, a petite figure broke from the crowd and threw her arms around his neck. It was Sidra.

"Thank God you're all right—I was terrified," she told him.

Geoff's response was to draw her more tightly to him.

If Elizabeth were jealous at this display of affection,

she didn't have time to show it before Lance grabbed her by the hand and dragged her away.

Lucy's progress was slower, hampered by the blanket she was clutching around herself. The crowd was already dispersing by the time she finally made it to solid ground, awkwardly assisted by Toby. She hadn't exactly expected to be hoisted on someone's shoulders and cheered by an enthusiastic crowd, but the general lack of enthusiasm at her triumphant return was discouraging. Even Toby promptly deserted her, hurrying off to tell his friends all about his adventures.

Spotting Horowitz conferring with a couple of officers, she went over to him.

"Can I help you?" he asked, impatiently.

"Uh, well, I just wondered when you'd be taking my statement . . ."

He raised an eyebrow.

". . . or whatever," she finished lamely.

"Thank you," he said formally. "I know where to reach you if I need additional information."

"Oh," said Lucy, feeling rather deflated as she crossed the parking lot to her car. She shrugged off the blanket Geoff had given her and folded it neatly, placing it on the backseat. Toby could return it to the Lady L tomorrow. Then she slid into place behind the wheel.

Being a hero isn't all it's cracked up to be, she thought as she started the engine.

At the *Pennysaver*, Phyllis welcomed her with a big hug.

"I heard the whole thing on the scanner. It's a miracle you weren't killed. They said if he'd hit a rock . . ."

Lucy's knees suddenly gave out and she grabbed the counter for support. Phyllis wheeled one of the desk chairs over to her and she sat down, trembling.

"This is silly. I don't know what's come over me."

"It's just a delayed reaction," Phyllis reassured her.

"The adrenalin's wearing off or something. Here, take some of this."

She handed Lucy the can of Coke that was sitting on her desk. Lucy sipped at it, waiting for the sugar to hit her bloodstream.

"Where's Ted?" she asked when she felt a little better.

"Over at the police station."

Phyllis had no sooner spoken than the bell jangled and the door flew open, causing Lucy to jump in her chair.

"So there you are! The hero of the day!" exclaimed Ted.

"It was nothing—" began Lucy.

"Give me eighteen inches," said Ted, cutting her off. "A first-person account of your terrifying ride. I need it by five. Tomorrow's deadline, you know."

Phyllis clucked her tongue. "I better get you something to eat," she said. "What do you want?"

Even choosing a sandwich seemed beyond her.

"What's the matter with you?" demanded Ted.

Lucy leaned back in the chair and closed her eyes.

"She's in shock; can't you see?" snapped Phyllis. "Put a blanket or something on her. I'll be right back." She marched out the door.

Ted reached for the old sweater that hung on the coat rack year-round and laid it over her.

"Does this mean you won't be able to work today?" he asked.

Lucy shrugged. Actually, the sugar and caffeine were beginning to take effect, and she was feeling much better by the time Phyllis returned, with Dorfman in tow.

"I'm a little confused," he began. "They're saying the harbormaster killed Davitz?"

"That's right. Frank Wiggins," said Lucy, taking a bite of chicken salad on white. It tasted great. She thought it might be the best thing she'd ever eaten.

"He always had a terrible temper," said Phyllis. "Even as a little boy."

"Poor communication skills," said Lucy, her mouth full.

"The job was way over his head," said Ted.

"So the theory is he just lost his temper and whacked Davitz?" Dorfman didn't seem convinced.

All three nodded.

"From what he told me, I think they argued over the fishermen's parade float," said Lucy, pausing before tackling the second half of her sandwich. "I saw him when it went by, and he was absolutely livid. I think he must have gotten into some sort of argument about it with Davitz. I don't know who started it, but he told me Davitz told him it was his own fault that the fishermen didn't respect him. His reply was to conk him on the head. When he realized he'd killed him, he tried to cover it up by rolling his body in the water so it would look like he drowned."

"And then he told the police he saw Geoff Rumford do it," added Ted. "The police were all set to arrest Geoff."

"Nice," said Dorfman, with a little whistle.

Phyllis snorted. "He always was a little weasel. I remember—this was years ago when he was ten or twelve, I guess. I caught him stealing my cat. When I stopped him he said it was lost and he was taking it to the shelter."

"I suppose it's possible," said Dorfman skeptically.

"Misty had a collar and was sitting on my front step at the time," said Phyllis. "I always wondered what he planned to do with her."

"He probably just wanted something to love," suggested Lucy.

"I don't think so," said Phyllis.

"They're sure he's the guy?" Dorfman still wasn't convinced.

"Oh, yeah," said Ted. "He gave a full confession on the boat ride back. Cops said they couldn't shut him up."

Dorfman shook his head. "When you think of all the people who had reason to kill Davitz, well, Wiggins is the last person I would have suspected."

Ted leaned back in his chair. "What exactly was Davitz doing? Some kind of pyramid scheme?"

Lucy and Phyllis were all ears.

"Kind of. It's called 'pump and dump.' He started out as a day trader and made some money, which he invested in this Secure.net outfit. When the stock suddenly began going downhill fast, he started planting hints in financial chat rooms that Secure.net was a real bargain and was going to go up. He touted the technology with a lot of mumbo jumbo, and investors believed it. They started falling all over themselves to buy it, and the price did go up. A lot. There was huge interest, and the fact that he was so reclusive just added to the stock's allure. The problem was, early on he'd announced the software would go on sale August fifteenth, but there was no software."

"That's why the wedding had to be early in the month," said Lucy.

"The honeymoon was the perfect getaway. He planned to cash out and ride off into the sunset . . . and never come back."

"There was never any technology?" asked Bill.

Dorfman shook his head. "Secure.net was a real company, some kind of home alarm system, that was practically bankrupt. The stock was selling for pennies when Davitz started hyping it as an Internet company. It's amazing what one man and a computer can do."

"And poor Sidra had no idea what was going on?" asked Phyllis.

"She thought he was the real thing," said Lucy. "But don't worry about her. She's going to be fine. Geoff Rumford is already making up for lost time." She paused. "Actually, it's Thelma I feel sorry for. He was her son, after all. She must have loved him."

"Don't feel too bad for her," said Dorfman. "The

apple doesn't fall too far from the tree. According to my research, she was accused of embezzlement back in the seventies. She was the volunteer treasurer for a charity thrift shop and she cooked the books. It never actually went to trial—the good ladies at the thrift shop dropped charges when she agreed to pay the money back—but the case is still in the court files."

"Was she part of this scheme?" asked Phyllis.

"I don't think so," said Lucy slowly, remembering how she had been struck by Thelma's odd attitude when she visited her on the yacht after Ron's death. "But I think she may have suspected something. She'd tried to call his company and hadn't gotten any response. I think she knew the jig was up and she was just trying to hang on as long as possible."

"As far as I know, investigators haven't been able to connect her with this scam," said Dorfman. "Ironically enough, if Ron had lived, they would probably have charged her as an accessory. He never would have gotten away with it, you know. I wasn't the only one who figured it out. The feds had cottoned on to him, too."

They fell silent, considering the damage Davitz had wrought, when the bell on the door jangled. It was Sid, wearing his fishing vest and brandishing a big manila envelope.

"Hi, everybody," he said, laying the envelope on the counter. "What's up?"

There was a pregnant pause. Lucy finally broke the silence.

"The wedding's off. Ron's dead."

Sid gave a long, low whistle. "When did this happen?"

"On the Fourth."

He furrowed his brow. "How's Sidra?"

"Geoff Rumford is consoling her."

He nodded. "And Sue? She was pretty keen on that wedding, you know."

"She's doing fine," said Lucy.

"That's good." Sid paused. "Hey, I almost forgot why I came here. You'll never guess what happened. I won the Northern Lakes Challenge," he said, opening up the envelope and pulling out a photo of himself with an enormous pickerel. "It's not just the biggest fish caught this year—it's the biggest ever on record. Almost five feet."

"Let me see that," said Ted, getting up and holding out his hand for the photo.

"I was kind of hoping you'd print it," said Sid, reddening.

"Wow. That's some fish. Sure we'll print it," Ted replied.

"That's not all," said Sid, producing a bronze medal in a plastic box. "I also got third place in the shoot."

"What shoot?" asked Lucy.

"The Northern Lakes Rod and Gun Club Annual Shoot-Off," said Ted, reading the medal.

"They have it every year, same time as the Challenge," Sid explained.

"So that's why you had a gun!" exclaimed Lucy. "Do you know how worried Sue was?"

"She didn't know about it. I never told her." He turned to Ted. "I knew she wouldn't approve."

"Sue found the gun," said Lucy. "She didn't know what you were planning to do with it, so she hid it."

"You know, you might be right." Sid scratched his head. "I thought I'd put it in my bottom drawer, but when it wasn't there I figured I'd just forgotten where I'd hidden it. I found it in my winter boots."

"Makes sense to me," Phyllis chuckled.

"I'd say you're the premier sportsman in Tinker's Cove," said Ted. "This deserves a feature story. What about it, Lucy?"

"Sure," Lucy said in a small voice. "I still have that first-person account to do, you know."

"Write that up today and we'll run the sports feature next week." Ted glanced at the clock and rubbed his hands together. "Well, time's a-wasting. We've got a paper to get out."

"Well, I guess I better get on home," said Sid, hitching up his pants.

"Hey, before you go, don't you want to know how Davitz died?" asked Lucy.

"An accident?" inquired Sid, cocking his head.

"Actually, Frank Wiggins killed him," said Ted.

Sid paused, scratched his chin, and considered this news. Finally, he spoke.

"You know, Frank's not very popular with a lot of folks, but I've always kinda liked him." He nodded his head. "Good man, Wiggins."

Chapter Twenty-three

"Nothing like a sunny Sunday," said Bill a few weeks later.

Lucy looked up from the newspaper she was reading at the kitchen table. It was just the two of them; the kids were all still asleep.

"We ought to do something special. It's a shame to waste a beautiful day like this," he said.

"What do you have in mind?"

"Let's go on a picnic. A family picnic, like we used to."

Lucy smiled, remembering expeditions in past years, when they had loaded up the car with beach chairs and umbrellas and inner tubes, plus a big cooler filled with sandwiches and cookies and fruit and lemonade, and headed for a nearby state park, where there was a lake for swimming, picnic areas, and hiking trails. It had been fun, but that was when the kids were much younger. Nowadays, they didn't want to hang out with their parents.

"I think the kids have already made plans," she said.

"When they hear the words 'picnic at the lake' they'll change them," Bill said confidently, pouring himself another cup of coffee and reaching for the sports section.

Zoe, as usual, was the first to wake up.

"Hey, Zoe, I've got a treat for you," said Bill. "A picnic at the state park!"

Zoe was fixing herself a bowl of Cheerios. "I'm going to Sadie's, today. She's got a new video game."

"Oh," said Bill.

Lucy didn't say anything, but buried her nose in the magazine section.

Bill was reading the business section when Sara appeared.

"Good morning, pumpkin," Bill greeted her. "I've got a surprise—a picnic at the lake!"

"Sorry, Dad," said Sara, reaching for the cereal box. "I'm helping out at the Friends of Animals car wash today."

"Hmm," said Bill.

He had moved on to the automotive section when Elizabeth rushed into the kitchen.

"I'm late, late, late. No time for breakfast. I'll just take some coffee."

"Where do you think you're going?" demanded Bill. "We're having a family picnic—at the lake!"

"That's nice, Dad," said Elizabeth, giving him a peck on the cheek. "I wish I could go, but I've got a date with Lance."

Outside, they heard a car horn beep.

"Gotta run! Have fun on the picnic!"

"Humph," said Bill, reaching for the real estate ads. He was studying the listings when Toby stumbled into the kitchen.

"Hey, Toby-my-man," said Bill. "What say we go fishing at the lake, like we used to? We could even take a picnic."

"Sorry, Dad, I want to see that new football movie."

This was too much for Bill. "You're going to spend a beautiful day like this *indoors*?"

Toby nodded. "I've been outdoors every day this

summer. It's not exactly a treat. At least the movie theater is air-conditioned."

Lucy thought she heard Bill growl. It was definitely not the time to say "I told you so."

"We can do something together," she suggested in a sweet voice. "Won't that be nice?"

Later that afternoon, they were sitting in the gazebo when a car pulled into the driveway. It was Sidra and Geoff, accompanied by Sue and Sid.

"See," said Bill. "Some kids aren't allergic to their parents."

"Hi," Lucy greeted them. "What's up?"

Sidra was bubbling over with excitement. "Guess what? Geoff and I are getting married and we want to use your gazebo. The justice of the peace is meeting us here in an hour—is that okay?"

Lucy blinked in surprise. "In an hour?"

"I know it's sudden," said Sidra.

"Not that sudden," said Geoff. "We've had the license for more than a week."

"It was just going to be a quiet family ceremony at home," said Sid.

"But then the weather was so nice," said Sue, "and I knew you wouldn't mind if we used the gazebo."

"Mind? I'm thrilled," Lucy said. "But we only have an hour to get ready."

"Calm down, Lucy," admonished Sue. "You don't have to do anything. This is going to be really simple."

"Right," Sidra agreed. "After all that madness before, we just want to say our vows as simply as possible, with the people we really care about as witnesses."

"What, no dress?" It was Sara, returning home from the car wash. Her hair was plastered flat to her head and her clothes were soaking wet.

Sidra laughed. "I always thought I wanted to get married in a long, white dress with a big, full skirt, but now I know it's not the dress that matters." She looked up at Geoff. "It's the man."

Lucy had an idea. "Come with me," she said. "Maybe you can have both."

In her bedroom, Lucy took the box containing her wedding dress down from the closet shelf.

"I don't know if this will fit you . . ." she said, lifting the dress out of its nest of tissue paper and holding it up.

Sidra's eyes glowed when she saw it. "It's beautiful," she sighed, fingering the delicate fabric. "But I couldn't. It's your dress."

"I'd love for you to wear it. Nothing would make me happier."

"Well . . ."

Lucy hurried downstairs, almost bumping into Bill in the kitchen.

"Where is everybody?" she asked.

"Outside, waiting for the J.P. I was just getting some drinks."

Lucy peered into the refrigerator.

"You'll have to go to the store. We need soda, and you can pick up a sheet cake. Try to get one that isn't too colorful," she said, pushing him out the door.

"Champagne glasses, champagne glasses," she muttered to herself, opening the door to the pantry.

Lucy was setting the glasses on a tray when the kitchen door opened and Zoe came in.

"What are you doing, Mom?"

"We're going to have a wedding. Sidra and Geoff are getting married in our gazebo."

Zoe's eyes widened and she started jumping up and down in excitement. When Sara thunked down the kitchen stairs from her room where she'd changed into dry clothes, Zoe grabbed her hands and started dancing with her around the kitchen.

"Enough, girls. I need your help," said Lucy. "Go out to the garden, will you, and pick every flower you can find."

The girls were shocked.

"Every flower?"

"Absolutely. And then you can make them into bouquets, okay? One for each of you and one for Sidra."

"What about me?" It was Elizabeth, home from her date with Lance.

"You can help, too. You can all be bridesmaids."

Giggling, the girls headed for the garden.

Lucy was filling a pitcher with ice when Toby came home.

"Toby!" she exclaimed. "Don't you have a boom box up in your room?"

"Sure, Mom. But the batteries are dead."

"Just bring it down, okay? We need it for the wedding."

"Wedding?"

"Just get it," she said, hearing the familiar crunch of tires on gravel. "I think that's the justice of the peace."

It was Bill.

"Thank heaven it's you," she said. "Where's that big extension cord? The one we use for the Christmas lights?"

"Gee," said Bill, setting the grocery bags on the table. "For a minute there I thought you loved me for myself alone."

Lucy peeked into the bag. "This was the best you could do? 'Happy Birthday, Zelda'?"

A hush fell as they gathered in the gazebo and Lucy pressed the button on the boom box. The stately phrases of Pachelbel's "Canon" filled the air, and they all turned toward the house.

First came Zoe, in her best summer dress. She was carrying a basket of dandelion heads which she scattered on the pathway. Kudo followed, the ring tied to his collar with a white handkerchief, scarfing up the kibble Zoe had cleverly mixed with the flowers to guarantee his cooperation.

Next came Sara, also in her summer best, blushing brightly as she tottered along in her first pair of heels. She was clutching a bouquet of zinnias and cosmos, tied together with cascades of curling ribbon.

Then Elizabeth appeared, quite a sight in hot-pink Capri pants and a pair of cool European-style wraparound sunglasses. Inwardly, Lucy moaned.

At last, Sidra stepped forward, a vision of loveliness as she floated down the path in the white wedding dress. Lucy heard Geoff's sharp intake of breath when he saw his bride, and she reached for Bill's hand, feeling his warmth as he gave her a gentle squeeze. Tears sprang to her eyes.

Sidra took her place beside Geoff.

The justice of the peace opened her book.

"Dearly beloved . . ."

"Who is Zelda and what is she . . . that nobody remembered to pick up her birthday cake?"

Geoff was beaming, standing with his arm around his bride and offering her a bite of cake topped with orange-and-blue frosting.

"I'm not wasting any tears on Zelda," said Sidra, taking a bite. "I'm far too happy."

"Hear, hear," said Lucy, passing around the champagne glasses filled with ginger ale. "We'll have a mock-champagne toast. To happiness."

"To love," said Bill.

"To true love," said Sidra.

"For years and years of happiness together," said Sue.

"What the hell is that thing?" said Sid, squinting at the sky.

They all looked.

"Could be a UFO," suggested Toby, a hopeful note in his voice.

"It's a balloon. Probably a weather balloon," said Geoff.

"No," said Sue. "It's a hot-air balloon."

"A silver hot-air balloon," said Lucy, hardly able to believe her own eyes.

"I don't know if I'll ever forgive you for not inviting me," said Norah, sipping some ginger ale. "I got suspicious when I saw the vacation schedule, so I called the town clerk and found out you'd gotten a marriage license. Then I had the research department call all the churches and justices of the peace." She shrugged. "I mean, what is a staff for, if you don't use them? Of course, getting the balloon was another thing entirely. That took some doing. They had to call all over the Northeast."

"I'm so glad you made it," said Sidra, giving Norah a hug. "Even if you had to come by balloon!"

"Oh, the balloon's for you and Geoff," said Norah. "My gift to you; it's going to take you to the airport where you'll depart on a European tour! Have a great time, kids."

"But we haven't packed . . ." protested Sidra.

"I have a thesis presentation . . ." began Geoff.

Norah waved her cake fork as if it were a magic wand.

"Trust Norah. Everything's been taken care of. Now, off you go!"

Geoff grinned broadly, then scooped up Sidra and carried her to the balloon, carefully placing her in the basket. Then he hopped in beside her.

"Cast off," he told the engineer, and the balloon slowly began to rise.

The girls ran toward it, jumping up and down. "Toss the bouquet!" they yelled. Kudo joined them, barking.

Sidra smiled and dropped it; Zoe snatched it from the air as it fell.

Geoff and Sidra waved as the balloon rose, and they all waved back, watching as it sailed off toward the distant mountains.

"That was the most beautiful wedding I've ever seen," said Lucy, tears streaming down her face.

"It was absolutely perfect," Sue blubbered, embracing her in a big hug.

Special Bonus!
Please turn the page and
take a trip down memory lane
with Lucy Stone as she relives
her wedding day!

"**M**om, there's nothing to do."

Lucy was standing in the kitchen, looking out the rain-streaked window. The leaves were already beginning to change, and the rain had made them glisten and shine like an Impressionist painting. It had been raining all day and everything was soaked through. The lawn was a soggy sponge, there were big puddles in the driveway. It was far too wet for Zoe to play outside. Inside, the house was unnaturally quiet. Toby and Elizabeth had left for college the week before, Sara was having supper at a friend's house and Bill was working late.

"I'm bored."

Zoe had wrapped her arms around her mother's waist and was leaning against her. Lucy stroked her soft, curly hair. Considering how busy she had been all summer, it was hardly surprising that Zoe was feeling rather lost. Lucy felt the same way. She missed the older kids, she missed the constant slam of the screen door as they came and went, she even missed never knowing quite how many there would be for supper. Zoe had loved staying up later than usual, tagging along for evening swims at Blueberry Pond and trips to Mr. Frosty for ice cream. But the highlight of her summer had been Geoff and Sidra's wedding, when she'd been a flower girl.

"I know," said Lucy. "Let's get out the wedding pictures."

Zoe went straight to the coffee table in the family room, where the packet of photos from Geoff and Sidra's wedding was lying among the magazines and clickers. But Lucy had something else in mind and was on her hands and knees in front of the bookcase. Finding what she wanted, she brought a big white photograph album over to the couch.

"Who's that lady?" asked Zoe, snuggling beside her and pointing to the photograph of a bride and groom that was on the front cover.

"That's me! Me and Daddy."

Zoe was not convinced. "Doesn't look like you."

"Well, it is," said Lucy, studying the photo of the picture-perfect bride with her long hair pulled back and piled on her head underneath the tailored bow that held her veil. She remembered posing for that picture: how her shoes had pinched her toes; how silly she'd felt in the stiff padded bra her mother had insisted she wear; how the dry-cleaning fumes from Bill's tux had made her feel nauseous under the photographer's bright lights.

Zoe pointed at the picture of the groom with her stubby little finger. "Is that Daddy?"

Lucy laughed. Bill did look rather unnatural with his pale, freshly-shaven chin and a glassy stare. He'd balked at a haircut, she remembered, and had tied his long hair back into a ponytail which had caused quite a stir among the older relatives.

"That's Daddy. He was very nervous."

Lucy opened the album and stared at the first picture, a formal portrait of the entire wedding party.

"Who are all those people?" asked Zoe.

"Daddy and I are in the middle. Then there's Jack, the best man, and Daddy's friends Doug and Steve. The lady in pink is my maid of honor, Debbie. She was my college roommate. The others are Corinne and Kathy."

"Are you still friends? They never visit."

It was true, thought Lucy. They had all been great friends in college, and had gotten together regularly for a few years afterward. But then marriages and jobs had taken them all in different directions.

"They all live far away and have families of their own. Jack came a few years ago—I guess it was before you were born. We get Christmas cards from them."

"Did you have a shower like Sidra?"

"Well, I had a shower, but it wasn't like Sidra's. Corinne organized it, in my dorm at college." Lucy smiled remembering how they had smuggled in a bottle of wine, which was against the rules, and how they'd stifled their laughter so the house mother, Mrs. Hopkinson, wouldn't discover them. No, it had been nothing like Sidra's shower, thought Lucy, remembering the gifts. "I still have some of the presents—the grapefruit knife, a vegetable peeler, and my Corningware casserole. And that pitcher," she added, pointing to a piece of handmade pottery she had filled with sunflowers.

"You always put sunflowers in that," said Zoe.

"I like the way they look," replied Lucy.

Lucy flipped the page and came on a photo of herself, posed in front of a mirror. Her mother was beaming at her, reaching up to adjust her veil. The picture had been posed and gave no hint of the tension between them that day.

"That's my mother. Your grandma. You probably don't remember her. You were just a baby when she died."

"She looks like you."

"You think so?" asked Lucy, shocked.

Zoe nodded. Lucy looked more closely at the photo of the trim woman with a shining cap of short hair and saw her own reflection. Of course, appearances could be deceiving, Lucy told herself. She was nothing like her mother, who had organized her wedding with a precision and authority a general could only envy.

She'd been an unstoppable force, remembered Lucy, who had envisioned her wedding as a simple statement of vows exchanged on a mountainside or a beach. Afterward . . . Well, she and Bill hadn't really thought about afterward. She'd guessed their friends would bring things to eat and a portable stereo and they'd have a party.

"Lucy, dear, that just won't do," her mother had said, upon hearing her plans. "Leave everything to me."

And Lucy had, being much more interested in spending time with Bill and her friends at college. She'd had courses to take, papers to write and parties every weekend. Periodically her mother would call to confer about the wedding plans and Lucy had listened, half-distracted, agreeing with everything. She hadn't realized what she'd gotten herself into until she was summoned home to shop for a wedding dress.

"Something simple," Lucy had suggested. "Those Mexican dresses are pretty that everyone is wearing. With flowers in my hair? I don't think I'll need shoes— I'll go barefoot."

"How original, dear," her mother had replied, starting the car and whisking her into the city, where they'd visited every bridal boutique between 59th and 72nd Streets.

Lucy soon discovered that none of the boutiques went in for Mexican cotton, so she settled on the simplest dress she could find. Shopping for shoes and a veil had taken another entire day and Lucy had escaped gratefully back to school where she soaked her sore feet and discussed the situation with her friends.

"She wants me to wear a wig thing," Lucy had complained. "A fall, she calls it. And she says I absolutely have to wear a bra."

The girls clucked in sympathy. They'd all burned their bras as an act of protest the first week of the semester.

"And pantyhose."

The girls were horrified.

Lucy had decided to wait awhile before showing them the picture of the bridesmaids' dresses.

"Look at the cake!" exclaimed Zoe, bringing Lucy back to the here and now. While Lucy had been lost in her reverie, Zoe had been leafing through the album.

She stared down at the picture of herself and Bill holding the knife, preparing to cut into the six tiers of white frosting topped with marzipan roses. At least there were no statues of a bride and groom, thought Lucy, admitting that her mother did have good taste. Everything had been lovely, everyone had said so.

Flipping back a few pages, Lucy found her favorite picture: one of herself and her father dancing. Pop had died of a heart attack some time ago, when the older kids were quite young. Lucy still felt guilty about the way she'd behaved when she saw him for the last time in the hospital, only half of her attention focused on him, the other half still back in Maine with Bill and the kids. She hadn't understood how serious his condition was; she hadn't believed he wouldn't always be there for her like he was at her wedding.

She looked at the photo and smiled, remembering how she'd faltered in the back of the church.

"Chin up," he'd whispered. "It'll kill your mother if you don't go through with it, but you can get an annulment tomorrow."

She'd laughed, he'd squeezed her arm and then she saw Bill, waiting for her at the end of the long, white carpet. She'd floated down the aisle.

"Where was your honeymoon?" asked Zoe, when they got to the photo of the car decorated with streamers and a "Just Married" sign.

"I bet you can't guess," said Lucy, pulling Zoe close for a snuggle. "It was someplace really special."

"Disney World?"

"No. We didn't have much money—we were just getting out of school. We borrowed a cottage from one of Daddy's friends. It was just a simple place, with an outhouse."

"It doesn't sound very good to me." Zoe wrinkled her nose. "Honeymoons are supposed to be romantic."

"Oh, it was romantic. We took baths in the lake, we walked on the shore, there was a huge stone fireplace and we stayed up all night talking and making plans for the future. It was perfect."

She kissed Zoe on her nose.

"That's when Daddy decided he wanted to be a carpenter and restore old houses. We decided we'd live in the country in a big old farmhouse and have four children and a dog. And a vegetable garden." Lucy paused. "So where do you think our honeymoon was?"

Zoe shrugged.

"Right here. In Tinker's Cove."

Zoe pushed the album aside and stood up. Facing her mother she put her hands on her hips.

"Mom," she said, in a disapproving tone. "You should have gone to Disney World!"

Please turn the page for an exciting sneak peek

of the newest Lucy Stone mystery

BIRTHDAY PARTY MURDER

Coming soon from Kensington Publishing!

Finally, a sunny day, thought Lucy Stone, wife of restoration carpenter Bill Stone, mother of four and part-time reporter. Thick, gray clouds had covered the little Maine town of Tinker's Cove for most of March. According to the weatherman, it was global warming that brought one cold, gray, sunless day after another. There hadn't been much warm about it, but it had certainly depressed everyone she knew, thought Lucy. But today the sun was shining and good spirits would be restored.

Lucy reached for her bright pink turtleneck and pulled it over her head, shook out her shining cap of hair and studied her reflection in the mirror that hung over her dresser. Were those gray hairs, she wondered, leaning closer for a better look. She ran her hand through her short, dark hair and gently grasped a handful so the sun that was streaming through the window could fall on it.

When did that happen, she asked herself. When did her hair start turning gray? And why hadn't she noticed? She considered yanking out the gray hairs, but there were too many of them. She would have to get some hair color. Or should she leave it be, and let her hair lighten naturally? She remembered her mother, who had always insisted her hair was as dark as ever, long after it had faded. No, she decided, she wasn't ready for the salt-and-pepper look.

As she turned her head from side to side, imagining the effect of the hair color, the shaft of sunlight fell on her face. Was that a little mustache she was sprouting on her upper lip? She leaned anxiously into the mirror. No, she wasn't sprouting a mustache; it was a series of fine lines. Little wrinkles, she realized, dismayed. And there were more, around her eyes. She'd simply have to be more careful to remember to apply moisturizer, she told herself, reaching for her favorite gray slacks.

She pulled them over her legs and automatically reached for the button, but something was wrong. Had she somehow twisted the waistband? She looked down and saw a little pooch of flesh protruding between the two sides of the zipper. She sucked in her breath and zipped up the pants, then fastened the button. She carefully let out her breath and the button held. Just to be on the safe side, she pulled a long black sweater on over the pink turtleneck. The effect was slimming, but she knew it was only a temporary solution. Summer was coming, which meant shorts and sleeveless shirts and, she gasped in horror at the thought, a swimsuit.

She was definitely going to have to do something, maybe exercise more or go on a diet she told herself, as she hurried out of the house and started the car. It was almost eight and she didn't want to be late for breakfast with the girls.

Calling themselves "the girls" was a joke—but the group of four women took their weekly Thursday morning breakfasts at Jake's Donut Shack very seriously. All married with families and numerous commitments, they had discovered breakfast was easier to fit into their busy schedules than lunch.

Pulling open the door at Jake's, Lucy headed for the corner table in the back where they always met. As usual, she was the last to arrive.

"We ordered for you," said Sue Finch. "Your regular."

"Thanks," said Lucy, slipping into her seat and reaching for the coffeepot. "I guess I'll start my diet at lunch."

"You're going on a diet? Which one?" asked Rachel Goodman, pushing her oversized glasses back up her nose. "I've heard that Zone diet is very good."

"Not if you care about your health," said Pam Stillings, adjusting her macrame shawl. Pam had gone to Woodstock and had never quite gotten over it. "You can't tell me that eating nothing but meat and cheese and butter is good for you?"

"All you ever eat is brown rice and tofu," observed Sue, checking her perfect manicure. Sue was a faithful *Vogue* reader and a borderline shopaholic.

"Well, I like it," replied Pam, tucking her long brown hair behind her ear. "And it's good for you."

"I like it, too. I like everything. That's my problem," moaned Lucy. "What should I do? I could barely get my pants buttoned this morning."

"It's all a matter of mathematics," said Rachel, picking up her fork and diving into a big stack of pancakes. Rachel had majored in chemistry before dropping out of college to marry law student Bob Goodman. He was now a partner in an established Tinker's Cove law firm. "You simply have to expend more calories than you consume."

"Exercise more and eat less," translated Sue, stirring some artificial sweetener into her black coffee.

"Look at her; she lives on nothing but coffee," declared Pam, digging into her bowl of oatmeal. "You do that and pretty soon your metabolism slows down to nothing. It's smarter to eat plenty of fiber. It makes you feel full."

"Well, if I'm going on a diet, I'll need my strength," said Lucy, as the waitress set an overflowing plate including a cheese omelet, sausage, home fries and buttered toast in front of her.

"It's not fair," said Rachel, who was frighteningly well informed. "Did you know that our metabolism slows down seven percent every ten years? Figure it out: we need almost twenty percent less food than we did when we were twenty."

Lucy resolved to eat only half of her omelet, and to skip the fried potatoes and sausage.

"That's not the only thing that's not fair," said Sue. "I'm starting to get wattles under my chin."

Lucy's hand reflectively went to her throat. Was it as firm as it used to be?

"The skin on the back of my hands is getting so thin," complained Pam. "They get all wrinkly when I bend my wrists back."

Lucy looked down at her hands. It was true, the skin wrinkled back like the Saggy Baggy Elephant's.

"Don't you hate that?" sympathized Rachel. "But what I mind most are my disappearing lips. Where do they go? No matter how much lipstick I use, they just seem to curl under or something."

Lucy extended her tongue, tentatively. Her lips still seemed to be there.

"No, the worse thing is that when I look in the mirror I look just like my mother," said Sue.

Lucy felt a shock of recognition.

"Frightening, isn't it? Not that I plan to follow in my mother's footsteps. She's addicted to plastic surgery. Just had her third face lift." Rachel shuddered.

"My mother weighed 250 pounds when she died," said Sue, who probably wouldn't hit the 120-pound mark on Doc Ryder's scale. "But somehow, I still look like her."

"My mother was in denial," confessed Lucy. "She

dealt with aging by just pretending she looked the way she always had." She paused, remembering. "She didn't."

"My mom smokes like a fiend and drinks like a fish," said Pam, shaking her head in amazement. "The only reason I can think that she's still alive is that her liver is pickled and her lungs are smoked like hams."

"Thanks for the image," complained Rachel, pushing her ham to the side of her plate. "I've lost my appetite, thank you."

"I guess the thing to do is learn from their mistakes," Lucy said. "Mom neglected her looks and got all washed-out looking but I don't have to let that happen. I'm picking up some hair color today."

The others nodded in agreement with Lucy, except for Rachel, who peered at them owl-like through her glasses.

"Don't you see what you're doing?" she asked. "You're all reacting to your mothers. Sue's mom was fat, so she doesn't eat. Pam's mom smokes, so she not only refuses to smoke, she buys all her food at the natural foods store. Lucy's mom didn't take care of her looks, so Lucy's resolved to cover her gray. We need to stop reacting. . . ." She paused, collecting her thoughts. Then she spoke. "Instead of reacting we need to formulate our own personal, positive paradigm for aging."

The others looked at her blankly.

"What is it with her and the big words?" asked Pam. "Can any of you guys help me out and tell me exactly what a paradigm is and where you can get one?"

They all laughed.

"It's a vision, a plan," explained Rachel.

"That sounds like an awful lot of work," observed Lucy. "Maybe we just need better role models. Someone positive." She thought for a minute. "Like Miss Tilley. How's she doing, Rachel?"

Rachel provided home care for Miss Tilley, the retired librarian who was the oldest resident of Tinker's Cove.

"She's great," said Rachel. "Same as always. You remember taking sociology in college? About inner-directed and outer-directed people? Well, Miss Tilley is the most inner-directed person I know. She just does what she does. You know, she eats the same meals for dinner every week?" Sue counted them off on her fingers. "Roast beef on Sunday, cold beef on Monday, chicken on Tuesday, shrimp wiggle on Wednesday, a chop on Thursday, chicken a la king on Friday and baked beans on Saturday."

"Actually, I didn't take sociology," said Pam. "And if I had, I probably wouldn't remember it anyway. But I guess I'm inner-directed because we have spaghetti every Wednesday."

"It just means that she doesn't care what other people think," said Sue.

"She's just herself," agreed Lucy. "There's nobody like her."

"That's exactly right," agreed Rachel. "For example, she likes to wear a certain style of shoe. She's worn it for years. Gets two pair every year mail order from the company. Well, they finally discontinued it. So she was looking through the catalog and these sneakers that light up when you walk caught her eye. For kids, you know. Well, she decided she had to have them. I told her they were for kids, that she'd look ridiculous. Didn't faze her in the least. She told me she doesn't have much excitement in her life anymore and she was going to get the sneakers. And she did."

Sue was incredulous. "She's wearing sneakers that twinkle when she walks?" she asked.

Rachel nodded. "She likes them so much she ordered two more pairs, in case they discontinue them."

"I'll have to stop by and visit," said Lucy. "This I've got to see."

"How old is she anyway?" asked Pam. "She must be getting up there."

"Actually, her ninetieth birthday is coming up." Rachel drank the last of her coffee. "I think she's feeling her age a little bit. Lately she's asked me to help her go through her closets and drawers to clean things out. She's also got a meeting coming up with Bob's partner, Sherman. He handles most of the older clients' wills and things."

"Very sensible," observed Pam. "After all, she can't expect to live too much longer."

"Ninety years," mused Lucy. "Think how much has changed in her lifetime. We've gone from long skirts and corsets to . . . Britney Spears!"

When they all stopped laughing, Sue held up her hand. "I've got an idea," she declared.

They all moaned.

"You're going to love this," she continued, gazing off into the distance. "Why don't we have a birthday party for Miss Tilley? A really big party, you know, invite the whole town. Have the high school band and the chorus. She could arrive in a fire engine. After all, she is the town's oldest resident and she was the librarian for so many years, absolutely everybody knows her."

"We could do a 'This is Your Life' show," suggested Lucy. "Bring back people from her past, successful people she encouraged."

"I don't know if she'd go for something like that," cautioned Rachel. "She's pretty reclusive; she likes her routine. She wouldn't want to miss her shrimp wiggle. Plus, she doesn't like attention."

Sue waved away that objection. "This is a woman who wears shoes that twinkle when she walks."

"I bet I can get Ted to put out a special edition of the *Pennysaver*," offered Pam, referring to her husband and Lucy's boss, the editor and publisher of the town's weekly newspaper. "A commemorative edition chronicling her whole life. It will really be a history of the town during the twentieth century."

"That's a great idea," exclaimed Sue. "Are you all with me? May twentieth will be Miss Tilley Day!"

She raised her water glass in a toast and they all joined in. "To Miss Tilley Day!"

If you enjoyed WEDDING DAY MURDER
and your visit to Tinker's Cove,
then please turn the page for a sneak peek
at the rest of the Lucy Stone mysteries!

MISTLETOE MURDER
The First Lucy Stone Mystery

As if baking holiday cookies, knitting a sweater for her husband's gift, and making her daughter's angel costume for the church pageant weren't enough things for Lucy Stone's busy Christmas schedule, she's also working nights at the famous mail-order company Country Cousins. But when she discovers Sam Miller, its very wealthy founder, dead in his car from an apparent suicide, the sleuth in her knows something just doesn't smell right.

Taking time out from her hectic holiday life to find out what really happened, her investigation leads to a backlog of secrets as long as Santa's Christmas Eve route. Lucy is convinced that someone murdered Sam Miller. But who and why? With each harrowing twist she uncovers in this bizarre case, another shocking revelation is exposed. Now, as Christmas draws near and Lucy gets dangerously close to the truth, she's about to receive a present from Santa she didn't ask for—a killer who won't be satisfied until everyone on his shopping list is dead, including Lucy herself. . . .

TIPPY TOE MURDER
The Second Lucy Stone Mystery

Between ballet lessons, Little League practice, carpooling her kids to school and a husband in need of attention, fourth-time mother-to-be Lucy Stone has more than enough on her plate this long, hot summer. But when one of her dearest friends vanishes, Lucy's soft spot for a solid mystery gets the better of her. Dinner can wait. Tinker's Cove, Maine's most irrepressible sleuth has a job to do. . . .

An afternoon walk was a ritual for Caroline Hutton

. . . until the retired ballet instructor took a detour into the woods and was never seen again. The case takes a turn for the worse when a local store owner takes a deathblow to the head with a video camera. Now, as Lucy's own seven-year-old prima ballerina rehearses for her debut, a murderer prepares for an encore. The devoted mother and sleuth knows she mustn't miss either performance. In fact, her life depends on it. . . .

TRICK OR TREAT MURDER
The Third Lucy Stone Mystery

It's October in Maine and everyone in Tinker's Cove is preparing for the annual Halloween festival. While Lucy Stone is whipping up orange-frosted cupcakes, recycling tutus for her daughters' Halloween costumes, helping her son with his pre-teen rebellion and breast-feeding her brand-new baby, an arsonist is loose in Tinker's Cove. When the latest fire claims the life of the owner of the town's oldest house, arson turns to murder.

While the townsfolk work to transform a dilapidated mansion into a haunted house for the All-Ghouls festival, the hunt for the culprit heats up. Trick-or-treat turns deadly as a little digging in all the wrong places puts Lucy too close to a shocking discovery that could send all her best-laid plans up in smoke. . . .

BACK TO SCHOOL MURDER
The Fourth Lucy Stone Mystery

It's back-to-school time in the peaceful town of Tinker's Cove, and for mother of four Lucy Stone, it isn't a moment too soon. But trouble at the local elementary school soon has the sometime crime-solver juggling family, job and night classes with another mystery to solve. And it starts with a bang.

A bomb goes off with the noon lunch bell, but not before all the kids are safely evacuated and Carol Crane, the new assistant principal, is hailed as a hero. But days later, Carol is found murdered and the most popular teacher at school is arrested for the crime. But Lucy isn't buying the open-and-shut case and decides to uncover the real killer. . . .

VALENTINE MURDER
The Fifth Lucy Stone Mystery

It's Valentine's Day in Tinker's Cove. And while the cupcakes Lucy Stone is baking for her children will have pink frosting and candy hearts, Lucy's thoughts aren't centered on sugary sentiments. She's barely arrived at her first board meeting of the newly renovated library when Bitsy Howell, the new librarian, is found dead in the basement, shot only minutes before story hour was to start. The agitated board members assume that Bitsy was killed by an outsider, until Detective Lt. Horowitz arrives on the scene and announces that the killer is among them.

Lucy was already aware that Bitsy's uppity big city ways rubbed some people in Tinker's Cove the wrong way. But she has a hunch that motives for the librarian's violent death run a lot deeper. From Hayden Norcross's elegant antique shop to Corney Clark's chic kitchen, Lucy relentlessly snoops into the curious lifestyles and shocking secrets of Tinker's Cove's most solid citizens—secrets that will plunge her into a terrifying confrontation with a conniving killer. . . .

CHRISTMAS COOKIE MURDER
The Sixth Lucy Stone Mystery

For Lucy Stone, the best thing about Christmas in Tinker's Cove has always been the annual Cookie Exchange. A time-honored holiday tradition in the little Maine village, the festive occasion brings together old friends and new to share laughter, gossip, and of course, dozens of the best cookies you've ever tasted. From Franny Small's chocolate and peanut-encrusted Chinese Noodle Cookies to Lydia Volpe's famous *pizzelles* and Andrea Rogers's classic sugar cookies, the sweets are always piled high.

But the usual generosity and goodwill is missing from this year's event which turns out to be a complete disaster. Petty rivalries and feuds that have long been simmering finally come to a boil, leaving feelings hurt and a bad taste in the mouths of many guests, including Lee Cummings who accused Tucker Whitney—the young, beautiful new assistant at the day care center—of stealing her recipe for low-fat, sugar-free cookies. But the icing on the cake is when Tucker is found strangled in her apartment on the following morning. Now Lucy's busy counting suspects instead of calories.

TURKEY DAY MURDER
The Seventh Lucy Stone Mystery

Tinker's Cove has a long history of Thanksgiving festivities, from visits with TomTom Turkey to the annual Warriors high school football game and Lucy Stone's impressive pumpkin pie. But this year, someone has added murder to the menu, and Lucy intends to discover who left Metinnicut Indian activist Curt Nolan deader than the proverbial Thanksgiving turkey—with an ancient war club next to his head.

The list of suspects isn't exactly a brief one. Nolan had a habit of disagreeing with just about everybody he met. He'd made a lot of waves with the Tinker's Cove board by first petitioning to have the Metinnicut tribe recognized—a move that would allow the Metinnicuts to build a casino—and then blasting the current building plans for not being true to his tribe's heritage. The very idea of a gambling hall in cozy Tinker's Cove raised bitter arguments on both sides of the issue. But could it have also inspired murder?

Between fixing dinner for twelve and keeping her four kids from tearing each other limb from limb, Lucy has a pretty full plate already. So what's a little investigation. But if Lucy's not careful, she just may find herself served up as a last-minute course, stone-cold dead with all the trimmings. . . .

WEDDING DAY MURDER
The Eighth Lucy Stone Mystery

Already juggling four kids' hectic schedules, a rambunctious dog, an attention-craving husband, and a full-time reporter job, Lucy Stone can't possibly squeeze in another responsibility . . . Or can she? When Sue Finch asks for her help planning her daughter Sidra's wedding to Internet millionaire Ron Davitz, loyal pal Lucy willingly dives into the world of white lace, roses, and chair rentals. What could be more perfect than a backyard wedding in the Stones' newly built gazebo?

Live doves and a hot-air balloon, according to overbearing social climber Thelma Davitz. But the groom's mother's elaborate ideas and constant complaints are the least of Lucy's troubles. With the nuptials looming along with her latest deadline, the arrangements are in utter chaos—and so is Lucy's investigative piece on lobsters. Meanwhile, Ron is making enemies at every turn, including the bride's father, several local lobstermen, harbormaster Frank Wiggins, and the Stones' friend Geoff Rumford—who still happens to be carrying a torch for Sidra.

When the groom's body is found floating beside his yacht, Lucy isn't convinced it was an accidental drowning. From the picturesque waterfront to Norah Hemming's mansion on toney Smith Heights Road, Tinker's Cove is awash with suspects. Now, fresh from planning Sidra's wedding, Lucy finds herself contemplating her own funeral as she launches the harrowing pursuit of a killer who will do anything to keep from being unveiled.

BIRTHDAY PARTY MURDER
The Ninth Lucy Stone Mystery

The whole town of Tinker's Cove is looking forward to the celebration marking former librarian Julia Ward Howe Tilley's ninetieth birthday. Sue Finch, Miss Tilley's closest friend, dreamed up the party idea—at about the same time Lucy decided *she's* not getting old without a fight. Noticing crow's feet and a potential jelly belly, Lucy's resolved to exercise more and purchase some heavy-duty wrinkle cream, asap!

That sounds like a plan—until Lucy realizes her daughter's fourteenth birthday bash, a coed sleepover, may turn her hair white overnight. What was she thinking when she'd agreed to let Sara have the party? Obviously she *wasn't* thinking about the hormonal rampages of young teens. On her mind, instead, was the shocking death of Sherman Cobb, the town's oldest attorney, an apparent suicide. His law partner, however, thinks Sherman was murdered.

Poking about in Sherman's papers, Lucy turns up an intriguing tie between the dead man and Miss Tilley.

Meanwhile Miss Tilley's own past has come back to haunt her in the form of a mysterious niece named Shirley and a biker great-nephew named Snake. Soon no one can get to see the elderly librarian because the brash, bossy Shirley says she's "failing." Is Miss Tilley in grave danger? Will Sara's party turn out to be a scandal? Now, as a killer's ruthless plan rushes toward a conclusion, Lucy needs answers fast—or else she and Miss Tilley won't live long enough to make a wish and blow out the candles on this year's birthday cake. . . .

Grab These
Kensington Mysteries